As the car flew toward them, Jude grabbed Felicia's arm...

They leaped out of the impact zone, falling onto the rough stone steps. Rocks bit into Felicia's elbows, and she banged her knee as they rolled aside. Jude encouraged their momentum, tumbling her farther away, putting his body on the impact side.

Were they clear? Would they be crushed any second by the out of control machine? Felicia closed her eyes, breath held. Braced for collision, her forehead pressed against Jude's shoulder with his arm held up to somehow shield her, she knew it would not be enough to save them.

Every muscle in her body tensed. A shower of grit peppered her cheek. Felicia squeezed Jude's bicep, the only gesture of thanks she could manage. He had done his job, put himself on the line for her, a professional sacrifice. Ironic that they'd be together in death, though they hadn't managed it in life...

Dana Mentink is a nationally bestselling author. She has been honored to win two Carol Awards, a HOLT Medallion and an RT Reviewers' Choice Best Book Award. She's authored more than thirty novels to date for Love Inspired Suspense and Harlequin Heartwarming. Dana loves feedback from her readers. Contact her at danamentink.com.

Books by Dana Mentink

Love Inspired Suspense

Desert Justice

Framed in Death Valley
Missing in the Desert
Death Valley Double Cross
Death Valley Hideout
Christmas Crime Cover-Up
Targeted in the Desert

Rocky Mountain K-9 Unit

Undercover Assignment

Alaska K-9 Unit

Yukon Justice

True Blue K-9 Unit: Brooklyn

Cold Case Pursuit

Visit the Author Profile page at LoveInspired.com for more titles.

TARGETED IN THE DESERT

DANA MENTINK

LOVE INSPIRED SUSPENSE

INSPIRATIONAL ROMANCE

LOVE INSPIRED® SUSPENSE
INSPIRATIONAL ROMANCE

Recycling programs
for this product may
not exist in your area.

ISBN-13: 978-1-335-58836-4

Targeted in the Desert

Copyright © 2023 by Dana Mentink

For questions and comments about the quality of this book, please contact us
at CustomerService@Harlequin.com.

Love Inspired
22 Adelaide St. West, 41st Floor
Toronto, Ontario M5H 4E3, Canada
www.LoveInspired.com

Printed in U.S.A.

This is my commandment,
That ye love one another, as I have loved you.
—*John* 15:12

To those who step in to be the hands and feet
of Jesus for the children of this world.

ONE

Felicia Tennison's hands shook as she idled the car on the side of the road. What was she doing? Everyone from her best friend, Nora, to her very-ex-boyfriend Sheriff Jude Duke would say she was making a dangerous choice. It wasn't too late. She could avoid the coffee shop and sit, calm her breathing, think the situation over, maybe call up Nora and talk about it. Ten months ago she might have done that, but the need to go it alone seared along her nerves like an exposed wire. Before the January car bombing that almost killed her, she'd been an extrovert, always in search of people and conversation. After her extended hospital stay, with nurses, doctors and therapists coming and going in a steady stream, she was a different person. Jude's abandonment hadn't helped, either.

A scattershot of questions unleashed in her mind as she opened the envelope again and slid out the small photo. It was a school picture perhaps, showing a child maybe five years old. She had brown hair, captured in two ponytails, and a tentative smile. It could have been anyone's child, no connection to Felicia whatsoever, except for two things. The tiny photo showed a dimple in the girl's cheek, low down, just one, left side. Felicia fingered the place where her own dimple surfaced when she smiled. Silly. A dimple didn't prove anything. Countless people had them.

The kicker was the message written on the back of the photo in spotty blue ink above an address.

Meet me at the coffee shop near Mule Creek tomorrow at two. You've got to save your sister. Please.

Her sister? What sister?
Then a scrawled signature.
Keira Silvio Mattingly, a name she'd never heard before.

Her fingers again found her cell and she was ready to dial her mother, Olivia, but her mom was helping a family member through an illness in Athens. She was not sure of the current time in Greece, so she decided to call the other person who had raised her.

"Uncle Abe," she said, just as it went to voice mail. Not surprising. Her uncle was the resident doctor at the campground he'd started years ago in Death Valley for medically fragile children. Early fall and winter was the time when the campground was hopping and so was her uncle. And anyway, she knew what he'd say—the same thing he always told her about her origins.

"You were abandoned in the outer lobby of a fire station. Your mother and dad were asked to foster you because of your heart condition. That turned into adoption because your parents lost their own hearts to a little freckled beauty. I got to go along for the ride when your dad died. Uncle Abe got promoted, so to speak."

The "freckled beauty" part always made her smile, since she knew she was not textbook beautiful. Thin and with buck teeth that had required braces, but her uncle had always made her feel lovely nonetheless. Though her adopted mother was gruff, Felicia was loved to the point where she'd never really considered trying to find her biological parents. Even during her rebellious teen phase, when she'd run away, she'd felt no desire to find her birth mom. Sure, she'd been curious, but there had been no hole that ached to be filled, no uncertainty about her own identity.

Until she'd returned home from a late kitchen shift at the Hotsprings Hotel the night before and found the envelope with the photo on her doorstep.

Left by whom? This Keira woman? Why? What did it all mean? She left a quick message on her uncle's voice mail. "I need to talk to you, Uncle Abe. I'll call you soon, okay?"

When she disconnected, indecision swept over her like a heat wave. Continue on to the coffee shop for the mysterious meeting? Go back home, research Keira Mattingly and wait to hear from her uncle? Drive to the address where the child might be living and try to find answers? Too many choices. Then there was the one that involved swallowing her mountain of hurt feelings and asking Jude for advice.

Having a sheriff at her side would undoubtedly help, but thinking about him knotted her up inside. Being unceremoniously dumped by a man who'd filled her mind with thoughts of love was more than mortifying. It hurt. Lesson learned and not to be repeated where Jude was concerned.

Instead she prayed, but still no answer presented itself. The October temperatures were on their way to the low nineties, and she wasn't sure if her recently purchased used Ford was up to the task of running the air conditioner, so she opened the window. A light-colored SUV drove by, and she got a glimpse of a man with work gloves and sunglasses behind the wheel. He hurried on.

She tried to simplify her stampeding thoughts.

Choice A or B. Turn around, or drive the remaining mile to the coffee shop? One minute ticked into five and the time slid to 1:40.

Go, her gut told her. At least she could drive there and sit, listen to Keira if she did show up. There was no obligation to become any further involved than that. But what if she heard something that would change her life again? Anxiety infiltrated her mind, but she'd resolved, while lying in a hospital bed all those months with tubes connected everywhere, that if she was released, she wouldn't let fear slow her down for one hot minute. "Coffee shop or bust," she muttered. Resolutely, she guided the Ford back onto the road and let the warm air dance across her face. The decision eased her rattled nerves, and she relaxed against the seat as she drove.

Turning on the radio, she fired up a Broadway show-tunes station and let the cheerful music wash over her. Ahead was an old cement overpass, glowing golden in the light. As she drove toward it, humming along, a flicker of movement from above tweaked her senses. Someone up on top of the structure? No, surely not. A bird or rodent seeking a vantage point or hiding place.

The shadow of the overpass blotted out the sun as she tried again to join in the song. The scrape of rock from above topped the radio music as she passed underneath. There weren't any loose rocks that might fall. Should she turn around and check? A dark shadow cut the sunshine. There was only a split second for her to yank the wheel sideways as something exploded through her windshield.

Jude Duke figured he was entitled to another cup of coffee since he'd already put in a full day's work as acting chief of police for the tiny town of Furnace Falls in Death Valley, and it was barely two o'clock. What would it hurt to swing over to the coffee shop to tide him over for the last hour of the shift?

Maybe it would be a quiet end to his workday, as it sometimes was in the small Death Valley town. He'd just decided to allow himself the caffeine bomb when a small boom from up ahead caught his attention. So much for quiet.

Adrenaline surging, he hit the gas. The overpass loomed into view, dust writhing along the ground playing hide-and-seek with bits of broken glass. His palms went clammy.

The tire tracks marked where a vehicle had skidded between the cement walls and plunged out of sight. He slammed to a halt and leaped from the driver's seat, pulse thundering as he ran until he saw a vehicle tipped into the drainage ditch that led the periodic flash floods away from the structure.

He sprinted to the front of the crumpled vehicle, boots skidding on the debris-strewn earth. The rear left wheel was off the ground, spinning, and trails of broken glass sparkled in the desert sun. A woman was sitting in the driver's seat with head bowed, arms hugging herself. "Inyo County sheriff," he called out. "Are you okay, ma'am?"

He shouted again and got no response. The car was lopsided, leaving the driver's door angled into the ground. He reached for the handle and yanked hard on it, forcing it open. She was still unmoving, chin on her chest.

"Ma'am, I'm…"

And then she looked up and his world tilted. Felicia Tennison. Was he hallucinating? No, it really was her—delicate profile, the sliver of a scar on her neck below the hairline, the lush fringe of eyelashes deepening her confused expression. It took a few seconds for his brain to resume control of his mouth.

"Felicia," he said urgently. "It's Jude. I'm going to help you."

His senses made notes—the gaping hole in the windshield from the hunk of rock that had been tossed from the overpass and had now slid into the corner under the dash. Most definitely not an accident. No sign of anyone lurking around. "Can you hear me?"

"Jude?" she whispered. "What...? Why are you here?"

The very same question he had for her. He was so relieved she was able to reply, he had to force his heart to simmer down. "I was on my way to get coffee. Were you hurt in the crash?"

She shook her head, but she might not be aware of her level of injury. He wrenched open the door the rest of the way.

"It's okay. You had an accident. We'll get you to a hospital." He radioed while she struggled to catch her breath.

"Something fell through my windshield." She looked helplessly around at her glass-strewn lap.

Not fell, he wanted to say. *It was dropped.* Instead he tried for sensitivity, asking a series of calm questions to assess her condition.

"I'm okay, lost my breath for a minute." She nodded, as if to convince herself. "But if I hadn't yanked the wheel…"

They both knew if the rock had landed a few inches closer, she might be dead. He still couldn't see anyone hiding or parked vehicles nearby, but he didn't dare leave her to find out. The arriving officers would have to be his eyes and ears.

She picked the envelope out of a pile of glass chips and unbuckled.

"Stay still until we get you some help."

Ignoring him, she got out.

He tried to hold her in place. "Felicia, you need to go to the hospital. After what you've been through…" His words seemed to light a fuse.

She turned blazing eyes on him. "After what I've been through, I'm not going to the hospital unless I jolly well decide I need to."

He was glad to see her fire, glad and relieved, but still… "You could have internal injuries, a concussion."

Without acknowledgment, she shook glass chips from her clothing.

He bit back his irritation. His only choice was to ease off, hands ready in case she collapsed, guiding her to his vehicle against her protests. "Get in my car."

"No, thank you." Polite and infuriating at the same time.

"Felicia, someone dropped a rock on you. Let's not give them another crack at it, okay?" he said in exasperation.

Her eyes widened a fraction, but she complied this time. He stayed by her side, watching until another squad car arrived. His commanding officer, Head Sheriff Gwen Detweiler, got out. She quirked a brow at him when he introduced Felicia. He hoped his expression was impassive, professional. After a quick briefing, Detweiler handled the investigation herself, scoping out the area while he stayed with Felicia. The medics arrived, and maddeningly, they accepted Felicia's refusal to go to the hospital after only a few moments of trying to persuade her.

Her car was photographed and a truck arranged to tow it to the evidence yard.

Detweiler returned, a muscle twitching in her jaw. "I got nothing. Whoever it was knew how to get away fast. Why are you on scene, Jude?"

"On my way to get coffee." He turned to Felicia. "Did you notice anyone on the road before this happened?"

Felicia twisted the silver ring on her finger. He knew it was the first thing she'd bought herself after her hospital discharge. *"To remind me about what I've survived."*

Tough, but in the sweetest way he'd ever seen in a woman. He blinked his inappropriate musings away. She told them about a guy in an SUV wearing work gloves who'd passed her before the incident.

Detweiler pinned her with a look. "Where were you headed?"

Felicia explained with incredible calm about a photo she'd received, with a mysterious meeting to be held at the coffee shop. The revelation set Jude back on his heels. Felicia showed them the photo, which only increased his astonishment. Why in the world hadn't she called him?

You know the answer to that. He was about as welcome in her life as a bad case of poison ivy.

"May I have the envelope?" Detweiler asked. "There's no proof that this accident and the message you got are connected, but it's too strange to be a coincidence."

Felicia pocketed the photo and dropped the empty envelope in an evidence bag that Detweiler held open. Then she stood waiting.

The head sheriff cocked her chin. "The photo, too?"

Felicia shook her head. "I'm sorry, but I'm keeping that one."

"Fingerprints…" Jude started.

"Will be on the envelope if there are any," Felicia said. "But you can take a picture of the photo with your phone. Like you said, there's no proof this rock-dropping incident has anything to do with the photo, right?"

A tight-lipped Detweiler took the picture with her cell phone. "Not a good idea to press any further into this until the police investigate. I'll send an officer to the address on the photo and sort things out right now. You should go home."

Felicia shook her head. "Funny how everyone keeps advising me how to handle my life just now." She avoided looking at Jude, staring instead at Detweiler. "I'm going to the coffee shop to see if Keira might by chance be waiting for me still." She got out of the car, stepped away from them and poked at her phone.

Detweiler moved close to Jude. "Your former girlfriend, right?"

Embarrassingly, his cheeks heated up. Was there anyone in the department unaware of his failed love life? "That's all over now."

"Not far enough in the past for you to be assigned this case. I'll put Fox on it."

Fox, the last cop Jude wanted to think about. "I can be professional."

Detweiler quirked a lip. "No doubt, but Fox will handle it."

"He's in court today. I'll take her to the coffee shop and fill him in later."

Detweiler cocked a brow. "Something's going on here. Don't get involved," she answered after a beat. "A ride only and an escort home. Do you understand?"

Still feeling a flush of discomfort, he nodded and walked to Felicia, who was tapping out another message on her phone.

She didn't look at him. "I know you'll say I shouldn't go, but I'm going to call in a favor and ask someone to come with me. Beckett has been great to me, but he's so busy. Maybe Levi or Austin. I just hope Keira doesn't leave before I get there."

His cousins Levi or Austin? Why did he feel offended that she would recruit them to help? "I'll drive you."

"No, thanks."

"Someone tried to kill you."

She blinked. "Maybe. Or it could have been a kid looking for some excitement."

"My gut says no."

"Maybe your gut's wrong."

"That doesn't happen often." *Cocky, Duke.* His default mode.

She allowed a half smile and shook her head. "Nora says you're wrong practically all the time."

Nora didn't hesitate to speak her mind. Putting his little sister and Felicia into the same headspace reminded him of another reason he'd cut things off. Dating the sister's best friend? Terrible idea, especially since he'd only recently gotten his sibling relationship squared away. "Nora talks too much."

"Exactly what she says about you."

He leaned a hand on the side of his car. "I'm offering a ride, that's all. Your car's a mess anyway."

"Thanks for pointing that out." Her brow puckered as she regarded the damage while the tow driver hooked chains to the wreck. "Poor Audrey."

"You named your car?"

Felicia's look was mournful. "She's the Audrey Hepburn. Classy and gorgeous, or at least she was."

He resisted the urge to chuckle at her whimsy. "Back to the issue. If it's important to you to get to the coffee shop right away, take me up on my offer." He hesitated. "Nothing more than a ride from point A to B and back home again."

"Why do I have the feeling Detweiler wouldn't want you to do that?"

"I'm on duty, and she approved it."

Felicia twisted her ring. "Jude, I'm not trying to be difficult with you or Detweiler." She turned those shimmering hazel eyes on him, and his stomach tightened. "I have a feeling I need to meet Keira, that she's going to tell me I have a sister."

"What if you're wrong? Maybe it's not your sister. Maybe it's just some mistake, a mixed-up plot of Keira's?"

"I have to find out." Her expression was grave. "If there was a chance you had a brother you didn't know about, wouldn't you do the same thing?"

He sighed. "I would."

"Thanks for telling the truth."

Why did he have to be so honest? Without another word, he hurried to the driver's seat. "I'm taking you, and I promise I'll stay out of it. Taxi service only. Deal?"

She huffed out a breath. "All right. A ride would be okay, I guess."

It might be okay, but he was already wondering how he'd gotten embedded in Felicia's business so completely.

Just a ride, he echoed.

What could it hurt?

TWO

Felicia didn't want to sit in the cramped front seat of Jude's squad car crammed beside the radio console, much less talk to the man, but she couldn't continue to ignore his flood of questions. It had to be purely professional interest, and she figured it couldn't hurt to have a police perspective. And that was how she'd decided to treat the situation. She and Jude weren't friends or colleagues, simply two people sharing a ride and discussing a bizarre series of events.

Though she was doing her best not to look at him, she noted the sprinkle of silver in his close-cropped hair that contrasted with his deep tan. Distinguished, she'd thought when she'd first seen him after being gone from Furnace Falls for a decade. Handsome, was her second conclusion, but he'd never need know that. After her arduous season of hospital treatments and rehab, they'd started dating…a blissful time, for her anyway, that ended all too abruptly after three months. Bewildering.

Their relationship had seemed so natural at first, after his loving attention during her healing process. She'd thought the dating was a continuation of that affection and care, a new chapter, finally, after she was whole and healed. She was no longer a patient. She could step into the role of honest-to-goodness girlfriend. She'd believed that right up until the rug had been pulled from underneath by their breakup three weeks before.

"You mentioned you were adopted, but you didn't know the identity of your birth parents?" Jude's question intruded on her thoughts.

"Yes. I was left at the entrance to the fire station. One of the firefighters spotted a woman putting me there. Young, a teen possibly. She wouldn't stay to answer questions. That's all I know. My mom and dad were foster parents and were asked to care for me after the social workers learned I had a heart condition that needed addressing. My dad was a doctor, like my uncle. They wound up adopting me formally when I was three, a few months before my dad died."

"But you were never contacted by Keira Mattingly before? Or anyone else about your background?"

"No."

"And you didn't look into it?"

There wasn't judgment in his tone, merely curiosity.

"Over the years I wondered, of course, but I had a mom and uncle, good ones, though my mother can be a tough cookie, which was part of the reason I skipped town with your sister after high school." He already knew the rest—that his sister, Nora, had been driving drunk, resulting in an accident that damaged Felicia's knee, ending her chance at a dance scholarship.

"That's an understatement, but Olivia's toughness helped her get through what happened in January." He grimaced. "Sorry. Probably not something you want to talk about."

"No." The ball of tension formed beneath her breastbone as it did whenever she considered how close she'd come to dying from the car bomb. "I trusted the wrong man just because I knew him in high school, and it almost cost me my life." Probably more evidence to Jude's mind that she was young and naive, thirteen years his junior. She straightened and clasped her hands together. "It took my whole being to convince Mom to go care for her sister in

Greece, so I'm not going to tell her about anything until I have a better grasp of the facts. The doctors say the cancer is in its last stages, so Mom needs to focus on Aunt Viv now, not me."

They arrived at the coffee shop, and Jude held the door open. She breathed in the scent of coffee beans and pastries. There were very few people in the shop, and she scanned each one of the women. A young twentysomething with two kids, an older lady working on a laptop. Neither showed any interest in Felicia. It was almost three. Had Keira left, thinking Felicia hadn't shown up? Or maybe the mysterious woman had never even been there in the first place.

Jude looked up a driver's license photo of Keira Mattingly and showed it to the barista.

He peered at the photo around a stack of mugs. "Yeah. I think she came in around two o'clock and sat for a while."

Felicia's pulse raced.

"Real jumpy," the barista continued, "which is why I thought she should lay off the caffeine. She left about a half hour ago."

"Did you see which way she headed? What she was driving?"

He shrugged. "Hey, man, I only dispense the beverages."

"Let's give it a while longer in case she comes back," Jude said. "I'll get us some coffee."

Great. Now she would have to sit with Jude and make small talk. But after he slid their coffees on the table, he busied himself studying every patron who came and went. They sat until her drink was cold and Jude's was gone, a solid hour, and there was no sign of anyone looking for Felicia. Had she missed her chance?

Unsure if she should feel relieved or disappointed at missing Keira, she let Jude toss the cups and lead her to his car. She noticed he checked the parking lot carefully as she buckled in. The memory of the rock smashing through her windshield made her shiver. He drove her back to her mother's house in Furnace Falls, as he'd done often in the three months they'd dated. Their time together had been easy, fun, natural, completely opposite of this strained silence as he walked her to the door.

"I...uh, I know you don't want to hear it from me, but it would be a bad idea for you to go to the address on the photo until we unravel the situation."

She fixed her gaze on the doorknob. "I appreciate your concern."

"It's not just concern, Felicia. It's common

sense. It could be that Keira lured you to the coffee shop for some reason. Or someone didn't want you to meet with her in the first place."

"I'll play it safe. I didn't survive an attempt on my life to throw caution to the wind now."

"Felicia…"

"Thank you for your help." She stepped inside and shut the door firmly behind her.

There was a pause before she heard his boots marching back toward his vehicle. He was frustrated with her, but that was no longer her problem. He'd broken up with her because she was too young, his sister's best friend, they'd wanted different things, et cetera.

You're not part of my life anymore, Jude. I don't have to make you any promises.

Jude strode through the golden October morning that was on its way to the low nineties—a far cry from the ferocious heat that would crowd in at the end of April. Life in the Mojave Desert. Old hat for the locals.

Detweiler had summoned him. Something that needed a face-to-face rather than an email or text. Ominous. He pushed open the door to the sheriff's office and was dumbfounded to see Felicia for the second time in as many days.

She sat in a hard-backed chair in the wait-

ing area, her expression dark. That was unusual. She was a glass-half-full kind of woman.
Somehow a degree of optimism had lingered
even after the bomb almost killed her and she'd
struggled through months of recovery. He realized with a lurch that she had one leg twisted
around the other, a habit she had that made her
appear younger than her twenty-seven years.
Why was there such a deep chasm between
twenty-seven and forty?

Heart thumping, he cleared his throat, and
she darted a look at him. "Detweiler called me
in."

"Me, too."

"What's going on?"

He didn't get a chance to answer before the
office administrator ushered them into a conference room. Mechanically he put out a hand
toward her lower back to guide her before he
stopped himself.

Not yours. Not ever.

He settled on pulling out a chair for her. That
wasn't proprietary. It was simply good man-
ners. Detweiler joined them. Only his long-
term familiarity allowed Jude to discern the
tension in her tight jaw, apparent in spite of the
iron control that was her hallmark. Her pant
pleats were knife-precise, silvering hair parted

neatly in the middle and captured in a bun, dark eyes intense.

She sat with perfect posture. "Thank you for coming in." She glanced at Jude. "Fox will be held up in court until tonight, so I'll brief him on all of this later."

"All of what?" Felicia leaned forward. "Why did you ask me to come?"

"We'll need more information, a few details we have to collect on the overpass accident, but there's…been a development."

Jude's stomach tightened. "What kind of development?"

Detweiler breathed through her nose. "Keira Mattingly was found dead last evening."

Jude stared.

Felicia gasped. "What? What happened?"

Jude's question, too, precisely.

"It's premature to say, but her body was found at the foot of Steel Rock Point."

Steel Rock, just outside Furnace Falls.

"Massive cranial trauma, or at least that's our unofficial read on the situation. The coroner will do an autopsy."

Felicia had gone pale. "Did she…jump? Fall?"

Or was she pushed? Jude wondered.

"That we can't say. What I can tell you is that we confirmed the child at the Mule Creek address is indeed Keira's daughter—Gracie Silvio, age six. Keira moved her in with a woman who used to be their housekeeper a few weeks ago."

"Keira and her husband were definitely on the outs," Jude said, "for her to do a thing like that." At Felicia's quick glance, he explained, "I did some research on her last night. Housekeeper says Keira didn't want Aaron around Gracie, but she didn't articulate her reasons."

"He's Keira's second husband. Her first was killed by a hit-and-run driver eighteen months ago," Detweiler said. "Aaron Mattingly called us at ten p.m. last night and reported her missing. He said she'd been acting irrationally, emotionally volatile. She allegedly told him she was going for a drive at seven, and he followed as she headed toward Furnace Falls, but he lost her. After a few hours of driving around, he called us."

"Can anyone corroborate his story?"

Detweiler shook her head.

Felicia had gone completely silent.

"Miss Tennison," Detweiler said. "In light of what's happened, I would like to ask you for that photo."

Felicia pulled it from her pocket and slid it across the table. "Who's going to tell her?"

Detweiler cocked her head. "Tell her?"

"The little girl. Gracie. Who's going to tell her that her mother's dead?"

The emotion in Felicia's voice plucked at his nerves. "Since there are questions about Aaron that need to be answered, we'll send a social worker," he said gently. "That's how it usually works when there's…no living parent."

"Who's going to take care of her? Aaron?" Felicia looked from him to Detweiler and back again.

"Since her death is suspicious, we'll need to look into the husband before we consider him." Detweiler straightened the folders in front of her. "Research will need to be done to see if Keira had a will or other legal direction designating guardianship."

Felicia didn't seem to hear.

Detweiler's phone buzzed and she checked it. "Unfortunately, I need to go now. I'll call you about other details. In the meantime, I wanted you to know Fox will be heading over to the Mule Creek home later this afternoon to collect some info, and he'll remain there until the social worker arrives." She cleared her throat. "If you think of anything else, something you remember about the car you saw before the accident, or any odd phone or text messages…"

"I'll let you know," she said.

Detweiler left.

Felicia stared at the closed door. Without warning, she stood and pushed her way out. Jude followed. He did not catch up to her until she hit the parking lot, where he finally grasped her wrist.

With no choice, she turned to face him. "I have to leave, Jude."

"Tell me what you're thinking."

She frowned. "This isn't your concern. *I'm* not your concern."

"Look, I know things didn't work out between us, but you're at a police station after you missed a meeting with a woman you apparently don't know and now she's dead."

"I understand all that. I will handle things my own way." She walked so fast to the visitor parking lot she almost tripped. He jogged along behind.

"You're in trouble, and you're planning something. You need to tell me what." *Bold, Jude.*

She stared back at him defiantly. Had he thought using his "sheriff" voice, as his sister called it, was going to work?

"Actually, I don't."

"You're going to go see Gracie, aren't you?" Even as he said it, he wondered at his forwardness. He had no right to intrude on Felicia's situation. She'd made it abundantly clear that she didn't want him involved. His sister, Nora, had told him recently, *"Grit's good, but it can rub people the wrong way."*

"No grit, no pearl," was Jude's motto. He pressed a little more. "I know you well enough to read the signs, Felicia. You get this crimp in your lower lip when you're determined about something. You're going to Mule Creek."

She lifted her chin in a challenge. "Keira said Gracie is my sister. Maybe Keira was my mom, too. I don't know if any of it is true or not, but I need to go see this child for myself. I can't explain it, and I'm not going to ask your permission. This is my decision."

"I can respect that. I'll take you."

"I…"

"You shouldn't go without a police presence. Detweiler would tell you the same. Fox won't get there until afternoon." Now it was his turn to wait. She could easily refuse, rent a car, enlist his cousins to help, call an Uber, but that would take time to arrange, and there was urgency emanating from her in waves. The seconds ticked by in slow motion.

"Just drop me off," she blurted out finally. "I'll get a ride back. A quick trip."

Victory. He nodded, hiding his relief. A quick trip, a short visit and then Fox would arrive to take over security. Maybe it was nothing to worry about, but something deep down told him Felicia needed his help.

Grit or no grit, she was going to get it.

THREE

She was relieved that Jude lapsed into silence as they drove, taking the off-ramp onto a road that wound through burnished foothills nestled beneath the towering mountains. A rabbit the same color as the ground peered at them from beneath branches as if curious about their purpose on the lonely stretch.

"This is a pretty out-of-the-way location," Jude said. "What I learned last night was that Keira and Aaron lived with Gracie at their home in Las Vegas until a couple of weeks ago. According to Aaron, Keira abruptly moved Gracie and their dog out without telling Aaron, and she wouldn't disclose to him where she'd left her daughter. He complained to the cops about it at the time, but there was nothing they could do since Keira was still the only custodial parent." He eyed the rippled rock as they drove along. "Does seem like odd behavior on her part, to take the child out of the home. If the marriage was on the skids, why not work through a divorce or move into a new place near the kid's school and friends?"

"Maybe she was scared of leaving Aaron, that he was going to hurt Gracie or her if she did."

"Motive?"

"Men don't need much of a motive to hurt women, do they?"

Jude flinched. "I also phoned a lawyer friend of mine, Dan Wheatly. Left him a message."

She shot him a startled look. "A lawyer? Why?"

"To advise on the guardianship situation until we figure out if Keira spelled out her legal wishes. Aaron had started the process to adopt Gracie several months ago, but it wasn't finalized."

"But if Keira didn't trust him…"

"We'll look into it, but we don't know if Keira's story is to be trusted, either."

Felicia's heart automatically turned toward believing the mother, but what did she know? Her poor judgment skills had almost gotten her blown up by a car bomb. *That's why he's a cop and you help rescue donkeys.* Her work with the Big Valley Donkey Rescue in Colorado had taken a pause while she recovered, but she was still on call to help Nora with relocations. She'd assisted with recently captured Bubbles and her new foal, Pinky, who stayed with Seth and Nora at the Roughwater Ranch. Two burros, Salt and Pepper, had found a home at her uncle's camp, thanks to Big Valley. Rescue work didn't pay enough to make a dent in her medical bills, so she'd required an immediate job upon her hospital release. She found herself content working at the Hotsprings Hotel for Jude's cousin Beckett Duke and his wife, Laney. Their daughter, Fiona (also known as Muffin), was a source of endless entertainment.

They'd turned upon a rough road that rose and fell along with the terrain. As they bumped over the rocky ground, Felicia tried to put thoughts of the overpass incident out of her mind. *Focus on why you're on your way to Mule Creek.*

Why was she? She couldn't put it into words any better than she already had…a driving need to see the child who might be her sister. Half sister? Was Keira mother to both of them, as her message implied? Was the whole thing some sort of scam? The last thing Felicia needed was to be drawn into another situation that would detour her from restarting her life. The muscles in her stomach tensed.

The last portion of the drive was a final hairpin turn that emptied into a steep section, the road pinched in on both sides by granite-flecked boulders. Jude rode the brakes during the sharp descent that led them to a tiny stucco-sided house, baking in the sunlight.

"Killer driveway." He put the vehicle in Park.

She gulped when he turned off the ignition. The moment had arrived.

Jude looked at her. "You sure you want to do this right now?"

Prickles cascaded along her arms. She was not certain at all, but that didn't matter. Instead of answering, she nodded and stared straight ahead. If the Lord wanted her to meet her sister, she wasn't going to let cold feet get in the way.

Jude engaged the emergency brake. There was no other vehicle present, which meant Fox hadn't yet arrived. A startled bird shot from the pinnacle of a rock at the highest point of the road, snagging Jude's attention. Scanning for any sign of what might have troubled the bird, he saw nothing.

He turned to open Felicia's door for her, but she'd already gotten out and was marching resolutely up the walkway, past the messy pile of terra-cotta pots brimming with prickly cacti of all description. The place looked like it must be under perpetual construction. Three dusty screens and a two-by-four with a strip of nails sticking out leaned against the garage door near a discarded bicycle tire. His phone rang.

"Sheriff Duke."

"This is Aaron Mattingly. I got your number from the station. They said you were involved with my wife's case." Aaron's reedy voice stabbed his ear. "What are you saying to my stepdaughter?"

"Calm down, Mr. Mattingly. I haven't spoken with Gracie yet. I'm sorting out a few details."

Aaron's voice was loud enough that Felicia could hear as well.

"Nothing to sort out that requires a cop," Aaron snapped. "It's taken me forever to chase down the address where Gracie's being kept, thanks to my late wife. I'll be there as soon as I can to collect her."

"I'm sorry for your loss, Mr. Mattingly. Are you Gracie's legal guardian?"

Felicia's eyes widened.

"Of course. The adoption paperwork has been started."

"But not finalized?"

"Why is that your business?"

"Because I'm a sheriff, and your wife's death is under investigation, so we've got to check into some loose ends." He kept his tone even.

"There aren't any loose ends. I'm on my way, and I'll make sure to have my lawyer contact you. I don't want anyone talking to Gracie."

The connection ended before he could say another word.

Felicia frowned. "There's something wrong here."

He didn't answer, but inwardly he agreed. They walked to the front door of the small house. A text appeared from Dan as Jude's knuckles hit the worn wood.

Coming to meet you at the address you gave me. Be there in a half hour.

Coming here? Jude wondered why Dan wanted to meet personally and at their current location. It would be an effort for the lawyer, since his legal blindness would require him to recruit a driver. The door was opened by a tall woman with a crown of iron gray curls. She leaned a hand on the door frame as if it hurt to stand straight. Her face was sun-speckled and void of much expression other than one…suspicion.

"Yes?"

"I'm Sheriff Jude Duke. This is Felicia Tennison. I left a message on your phone that we were coming."

"There have been a lot of messages this morning." Her gaze traveled from him to Felicia and settled somewhere between them.

"Are you Vera Zimmer?"

She nodded.

Jude glanced past her into the hallway to the cluttered family room. He spotted a coloring book and crayons piled on a chair. This was the place, he figured.

"We're here about a child, Gracie Mattingly."

"Gracie Silvio," Vera corrected sharply. She dropped her volume and pulled the door a bit more closed. "I understand why a cop would be here, since I've been informed that Keira has died." Her mouth trembled. "A terrible shame."

It was. Accident or murder? Jude still felt the shadow of the recent attack on Felicia. Hairs prickled on his neck as if they were being watched. Something in Aaron's phone call bothered Jude. *What are you saying to my step-daughter?* As if he knew Jude and Felicia were at Vera's property that very moment. "Would you mind if we came inside for a short talk?"

Now Vera's eyes traveled to Felicia and lingered there, a puzzled expression crinkling her brows. "Okay, but Gracie's resting, so keep your voices down." She ushered them into the messy room Jude had been surreptitiously checking out over her shoulder. A slipcovered sofa faced a small television. The end tables were stacked with gardening books, mystery novels and balls of yarn. She did not offer them a seat. She turned to stare at Felicia, mouth pursed into a small knot.

"Why are you here?" she demanded.

"I…received a message that Gracie is possibly my sister."

"A message? From whom?"

"I'm not sure, but I believe it was from Keira."

Vera went silent, absently picking up a ball of rust-colored yarn and squeezing it.

"Can you tell me how Gracie came to be living with you?" Jude asked.

"Like I explained to somebody named Detweiler on the phone, I was Keira's housekeeper when she was married to Luca Silvio. I stayed on after she remarried, but her new husband, Aaron, accused me of stealing. I didn't steal anything." Her voice was knife-edged. "But someone planted cash in my bag. Keira didn't want to believe it, either, but Aaron threw such a fit she let me go. I was never a nanny, never really wanted to be, but when Keira called me two weeks ago and begged me to keep Gracie for a little while, I said yes. Not because it was convenient, mind you, but because Aaron is bad. I know it in my bones and Keira was afraid of him. He has evil intentions where Gracie is concerned." She tossed the ball of yarn into an overflowing basket.

Felicia spoke before Jude could. "What do you mean, evil intentions?"

She shrugged. "I don't know exactly, Keira wouldn't be specific, but she pleaded with me to keep Gracie here until she could make better arrangements. She was going to divorce Aaron, I surmised, but she was afraid to tell him."

"What about school for Gracie? Her friends?" Jude asked. "Why move her here?"

"She's in delicate health, so I've been homeschooling her. She's a very quiet child. Not too many friends, from what I gathered from Keira. And anyway, this was supposed to be a shortterm thing. It's been very hard, since driving is almost more than I can manage, and Gracie has regular doctor's appointments and such. Then there's that big galoot of a dog." Vera blinked and Jude wondered if it was to whisk away tears. "But now Keira's dead, and everything has changed."

"Can I see her?" Felicia said suddenly.

Vera folded her arms and looked at the floor. A ball of yarn fell from the basket and rolled across the floor. "I'm not sure what to do."

Felicia picked it up and offered it to Vera, who did not reach for it.

"I was adopted as a baby," Felicia said. "I didn't know I had any biological relatives, but the photo Keira, or someone, sent to me has made me think maybe Gracie is some relation to me. I just want to meet her. I won't mention our possible relationship, I promise."

Vera looked past her. "I guess the decision's been made."

Felicia whirled suddenly, eyes wide.

A young child with braids walked into the hallway, followed by an enormous, spotted Great Dane. The little girl was pale, brown eyes contrasting with the pallor. An adhesive bandage poked out of the top of her pink pajamas.

Jude's breath hitched one notch as he let the resemblance wash over him. She had the same delicate bones as Felicia, the hair that curled at the temples. The dog suddenly bounded over, so tall he could almost look Felicia in the eye. Jude took a step to intercept, but the dog was friendly, dropping down on comically long front legs to offer his rump for scratching. Jude complied. "You're a tall drink of water, aren't you, fella?"

The dog accepted the attention for a moment from him and Felicia before he scrambled back to the girl's side and slurped a tongue over her cheek. The animal's coat was a splattering of white and black, and his saggy ears and jowls flapped when he moved. Jude wondered how the critter got all those enormous parts moving in unison.

"This is Gracie, and of course you've met Stretch," Vera said.

Felicia smiled and waved. Jude followed suit. Gracie wiggled her fingers at them.

He was about to say more when Vera hurried to the child, scolding gently. "You shouldn't be out of bed. Come on. Let's get you tucked back in."

They vanished, and Vera returned after a few moments. "She's had a surgery recently, and she's supposed to rest for several hours each day. With everything that's happened, she hasn't been sleeping well at night."

"What kind of surgery?" Jude asked.

Felicia spoke as if she was in a dream. "It was to repair a heart valve, wasn't it?"

Jude and Vera stared at her.

"How…did you know that?" Vera said.

Felicia blinked, touching her own chest. "Because I had the same surgery around her age. I was born with a narrowing of the aortic valve." Her eyes found Jude's. He didn't need any words to know what she was thinking. The evidence that the two were related was piling up.

A timer beeped from the kitchen. Vera shook herself. "Gotta get the next load of laundry started. Be a while."

"We'll talk in the yard for a few minutes."

Vera seemed relieved that they would not be trying to chat with Gracie in her absence.

Jude led Felicia outside. They stood in the shade of the house, next to the splintery garage door. He eyed the steep, plunging road. Empty and still. A gleam snagged his attention from the foliage. He stared but there was nothing there, only the flicker of dry leaves in the hot breeze.

A message buzzed on his phone. "It's from the social worker."

"What's the message?"

Felicia was petite, and her chin tipped back to take in his full six feet and change. He found he did not want to tell her what might happen. How could he deliver the facts softly, like she would? He was still standing there hemming and hawing when she squeezed his wrist.

"Jude?"

"Until we have a clear legal direction here, they may need to place Gracie somewhere temporarily."

Horror infused her face. "You mean foster care? But she's fine right here, and she just lost her mother. Won't they let her stay with Vera?"

"That might be an option, but Vera seems to be struggling physically, so I'm not sure. I have a feeling Aaron is going to object. This is up to the social worker. She'll be here soon."

"Then I need to wait to talk to her, tell her Gracie has to stay with Vera. She's recovering from a heart valve repair. It's not good for her to be carted off to some stranger, especially now." She turned to go back inside.

He stopped her with a hand on her shoulder. "Felicia, I know this is tough…"

"Tough?" Tears shone in her eyes. "That little girl has lost her mother, whether or not she knows it, and the guy who wants to adopt her isn't sending off warm and fuzzy vibes. I can't just sit by while she's dragged off with her stuff in a bag." She reached up and put her palm on his chest, immobilizing him. Suddenly his breath got short and his brain went fuzzy.

"Please," she half whispered.

Engine noise distracted him. He looked up and saw a red Mercedes turn down the steep drive. "That's…" His words died away as the front tires exploded with a pop. Rubber ribboned everywhere in ragged strips. In a split second the Mercedes careened out of control down the steep drive, headed right for them.

FOUR

The Mercedes streaked forward like a red comet. Felicia stared at the shimmying car, trying to make sense of it. The driver appeared to be attempting to brake, but the sharp incline of the slope and the two ruined front tires prevented it. She could make out Nora behind the wheel, face caught in a flash of sunlight. The passenger was male, one arm braced against the dash as if he could somehow slow the car.

The brakes squealed as the vehicle loomed closer every moment. It all seemed to happen at once, like a video playing in slow motion before her stunned eyes. The front bumper lurched within a couple of feet of the garage door, and she could see Nora clearly now, fingers white on the steering wheel. Try as she might, Nora could not stop the wild progress. Felicia's pulse pounded for her friend. The reality hit home. She and Jude were about to be crushed between the car and the garage. As the wheels spun closer, Jude broke her paralysis by grabbing her arm. They leaped out of the impact zone, falling onto the rough stone steps. Rocks bit into her elbows, and she banged her knee as they rolled aside. Jude encouraged their momentum, tumbling her farther away, putting his body on the impact side.

Were they clear? Would they be crushed any second by the out-of-control machine? What about Nora and her passenger? Felicia closed her eyes, breath held, thinking about her mother, how she'd stood beside Felicia every moment of her recovery, ferocious in her dedication. Felicia had needed to use all her will to convince her mom she should go to Greece and tend to her sister. Her mother would blame herself for leaving town, no matter the circumstances.

Braced for impact, her forehead pressed against Jude's shoulder with his arm held up to somehow shield her, Felicia knew it would not be enough to save them. She squeezed his biceps, the only gesture of thanks she could manage. He had done his job, put himself on the line for her, a professional sacrifice. Ironic that they'd be together in death, though they hadn't managed it in life. Every muscle in her body tensed. The Mercedes suddenly veered, and a shower of grit peppered her cheek. Felicia opened her eyes.

Nora had been able to yank the steering wheel, sending the car into a lateral skid. It was enough of a turn that the side of the car hit the corner of the garage with a deafening crash and was deflected away from the house. It was several moments before Felicia realized Nora's actions had taken them out of the crash zone. The correction had saved them both.

Smashing into a trash can adjacent to the garage, the Mercedes finally ground to a stop a few feet from a stack of yellowed newspapers.

Jude leaped to his feet as she sat up, breathing hard.

He took her hand. "Are you okay?"

She'd forgotten how blue his eyes were, or maybe she'd forced it from her memory. With a big inhalation, she pulled her hand away and nodded. "Fine."

"Sit tight for a minute," he said, whirling toward the crashed car. Instead she eased to her feet, amazed that the only pain she felt was from her scraped elbow and banged-up knee.

"Thank You, God," she whispered, anxious to get to her friend.

Jude reached the Mercedes first. Nora got

out and waved her brother off. "I can't even believe this."

"Are you sure you're okay?" Jude panted as Felicia jogged up.

"Completely." They all turned their attention to the passenger.

He was a sandy-haired man who moved stiffly, his palm on the car roof to steady himself as he got out. Jude and Nora helped him, and he assured them he was fine.

Nora squeezed Felicia tight. "I could have killed you. I've never been so scared in my life. Are you okay?"

Felicia hugged her back. "A-OK. But you might be hurt and not know it."

"The car took the punishment, not me or Dan."

Vera hobbled out onto the front walk. "What happened?"

Jude called to her. "A car accident. Please go back in the house with Gracie, okay? Be there in a few minutes."

Muttering, Vera took in the damage to the edge of her garage as she trudged back inside.

Nora stared at the ruined Mercedes. "Something in the road blew out both front tires, and I couldn't control the car."

Jude scanned the terrain carefully. "Give me

a second." He paced up the road, disappearing behind the rocks. Felicia's breath hitched. What if someone was out there? Waiting?

Jude was armed and trained, she scolded herself. He was more than capable.

Nora patted the roof of the crumpled vehicle and reached inside to retrieve something. "Aww, Dan. Sorry I wrecked your ride. You're not gonna invite me to be your chauffeur ever again, are you?"

The man took the cane she handed him, and Felicia realized he must be visually impaired. "No sweat," he said. "Cars can be replaced. Anybody hurt?"

"Only a scrape or two," Felicia said.

Nora introduced Felicia.

"Relieved to hear it." Dan extended a hand. "I'm Dan Wheatly. I'm a lawyer based in Furnace Falls. Don't think we've met."

"No, we haven't. Sorry it's under these circumstances. Are you sure you're not hurt at all?"

Dan waved a hand. "The power of seat belts. What in the world did we run over?"

Jude appeared at the side of the road and hiked back toward them. He held up a board between his two hands. The wood was weathered and worn, and protruding from it was a row of rusted nails. "This was leaning against the garage door when we got here. Found it in the road covered with leaves. My guess is someone drove up around the time we did. Probably someone watching through binoculars."

"But who would target me and Dan?" Nora said. "No one even knew we were coming."

"You weren't the target." His jaw tightened. "Whoever it was didn't want me or Felicia to get out of here safely, so they snagged this and laid it across the road. Improvised with what they could find. Probably hoping we'd have a blowout that would send us smashing back into the house, enough to injure or maybe just to rattle us."

"Yeah, but instead they wiped us out." Nora fisted her hands on her narrow hips. "Who's responsible and where did they go?"

Jude looked thoughtful. "The question of the hour. I called it in. Photographed everything, but the social worker is coming, so I couldn't leave it in place on the road." He turned to Dan. "Sorry you two got caught up in a crude plan to cause problems for us."

Us, or me? Felicia thought.

Nora's brow knit. "Why would anyone want to harass you for coming here?"

"I'm not sure," Felicia said.

Jude shook his head. "Let's go inside and work that out."

"All right." Dan put a hand on Nora's shoulder as they walked.

Nora groaned, taking in the wrecked car one more time. "What a waste of a beautiful vehicle."

Dan laughed. "Time to upgrade, I guess. Nora was doing me a favor since my regular driver had a dental emergency." He tipped his face in Felicia's direction. "If I may ask, what prompted you to come to this house with Jude right now?"

She saw no reason to conceal anything, so she told him about the photo. "It was left on my porch, so I didn't see who delivered it."

"When?"

She told him.

His brows puckered. "Interesting."

She was going to ask him why he'd come to the house instead of making a phone call, but he pressed a button on his watch and a computerized voice spoke the time to him. "There's something important we need to discuss before the social worker gets here."

Jude frowned. "What?"

Dan hesitated. "This is probably a sit-down conversation."

Felicia and Jude exchanged a startled look.

Then Jude nodded and knocked on the door again. After the introductions were over, he gave Vera a curtailed version of the situation.

"Any guesses who might have booby-trapped the road?" he asked.

Vera huffed. "Are you kidding? I don't need to guess. It was Aaron Mattingly."

"What would be his motive?"

"He wants to get his hands on Gracie, to adopt her. I don't know why for certain, but I'm guessing there's money in it. Isn't that what makes the world go around these days?"

"Why would he need to arrange an ambush?" Jude's voice was low, steely. "Aaron's Keira's husband, so he's already entitled to a portion of her estate."

"That's where I come in," Dan said. "This is the part where we all need to sit down."

Nerves prickled along Felicia's spine. Why did she have the feeling her life was about to change again?

Jude checked his phone. A follow-up text from the social worker indicated she'd arrive within the hour. He warned her of the potential danger and insisted she join the responding sheriff in town and travel with him. A few more texts and the meeting was arranged.

Vera led them to the family room again, clearing off chairs. She provided antiseptic and a bandage for Felicia's bloody elbow. When Vera announced her intention to leave, Dan stopped her. "You have a right to know what's going on, Mrs. Zimmer. Keira entrusted her daughter to you."

"I'm just the maid and cook."

"You've been much more than that to Gracie," Dan said softly.

Vera blinked and her mouth twisted for a moment. "I haven't been the best stand-in for a mother, but I've tried."

"Please stay and join us," Dan said.

She shook her head. "No. This is too much. I didn't ask for any of this, and suddenly I've got social workers and cops and lawyers trooping through my home, and it's upsetting. Now I've got a busted-up garage on top of it."

Jude sympathized. When life took a turn for the worse, he retreated to his isolated cabin, which he'd been painstakingly restoring after a violent attack on his cousin Willow left it in tatters. There he found peace, just him and God. No demands. No visitors. Not ever. The very moment the repairs were finished, he intended to hole up there for a good long vacation. "You're included in as much as you want to be, Ms. Zimmer. No pressure either way." That sounded like a sensitive comment Dan would make. He caught Felicia's quick, approving glance, which made him pleased he'd said it.

Vera huffed out a breath. "I don't want to be involved in whatever you're discussing. You'll tell me what you all decide. I've got laundry to do, and Gracie needs her meds. That mountain of a dog won't leave her side, so I'll have to work around him as usual. He eats more than Gracie and me combined." She clomped away.

"All right." Jude heaved out a breath. "Let's have it, Dan. You'll likely have to repeat all this to the investigating sheriff and social worker, but I'd appreciate hearing it firsthand. Felicia has a right to be in on it also, after the morning she's had."

Felicia didn't quite look at him, but he saw color rising in her cheeks. Had that been too mushy? Was there such a thing as being too sensitive? He wasn't sure if he'd embarrassed her or said the right thing. He never knew, where women were concerned.

Dan straightened in his chair. "I called Nora to drive me out as soon as you contacted me about Keira's death and asked me to weigh in on the custody situation. I wish I could have spoken to you instead of leaving a voice mail, and I could have front-loaded you both. I left messages on your phone for you to call me immediately."

Jude shifted. "Yeah, uh, sorry I didn't return your call. It's been a busy day."

"You are the worst at returning phone calls," Nora said.

Jude glared at her. "Busy."

"You don't return them even when you're not busy," she countered.

He was rallying a defense when Dan held up his palms. "The point is, when I couldn't get hold of you, I figured the next best thing was to meet you here since you mentioned you were headed to see Gracie." He paused, thinking.

Jude had known since high school that Dan was a sensitive man, and he measured his words carefully. As much as he burned to learn the facts, he held his tongue and waited.

"This is…unusual, but I'm the only lawyer in the immediate area, so I guess there's some sense to it."

"What?" Felicia said. "Why did you come here, Dan?"

Dan cleared his throat. "Keira showed up at my office just before closing last night."

Felicia gasped. "She did?"

"Yes, Wednesday evening."

The same day she'd tried to meet Felicia at the coffee shop. The same night she'd died.

"She was agitated, obviously anxious. She checked the window several times, as if she was worried someone would know she'd come to me."

It took all of Jude's self-control not to fire a half dozen questions at Dan.

Nora considered. "Keira was obviously scared. Dan's office faces the main drag. Entirely possible someone might drive by and see her, I suppose."

"You were there, too?" Jude demanded.

Dan nodded. "I'll get to that in a minute. Keira asked if she could close the blinds, and I agreed, of course. She had an urgent matter she wanted to address—a codicil to her will. The topic was the legal guardianship of her daughter, Gracie."

Felicia was on the edge of her seat now.

Jude furiously jotted notes in his phone, the electronic brain he now relied on to capture details his mind couldn't seem to hold anymore. "Go on."

"Keira did not want the child adopted by Aaron Mattingly. She didn't tell me why, but she was very clear. She insisted I draw up papers immediately to assign legal guardianship in the event of her death. She'd looked me up in the phone book, she said, and I was the closest lawyer to Mule Creek, where her daughter was staying. It was late, almost six, and I called Nora in since she's a notary."

"Why didn't she contact the lawyer who handled her trust?" Jude asked.

"I inquired about that, but she cut me off. She said time was of the essence, and if I couldn't help her, she'd drive until she found a lawyer who would. That wasn't likely to happen at such a late hour. I actually called the office of her existing lawyer in Las Vegas out of curiosity, but his office was closed on Wednesday evenings, so that checked out. It could have been a timing issue."

Jude calculated. The chance of finding a lawyer open evenings, even if she drove to the nearest big city of Las Vegas, was next to zero. If she'd needed it done that very evening, she'd have looked up the closest lawyer. Wednesday Keira contacted Dan. Later that night, she was dead.

Nora frowned. "She was about to jump out of her skin by the time we finished. Her hands shook for the signature part. The moment, and

I mean the very moment, we were done, she wrote out a check and bolted."

"And the evening before, she must have left the envelope on my porch asking to meet," Felicia said. "I was working late at the Hotsprings, and it was on my doorstep when I got home."

"Did Keira come back, Dan? Contact you further?" Jude asked.

"No. I didn't hear from her again." Dan sighed. "I was made aware of her death when you left a message and asked me to advise on how the guardianship might go."

Felicia bit her lip. "So Keira didn't want Aaron to have Gracie, and she made it official."

Jude mulled it over. "All the more reason to scrutinize his life closely. Motive here? Is there a sizable inheritance?" Had to come down to the dollars and cents. It most often did.

"That's the part I can't help you with, at least right now."

Jude shot him a look. "But you're her lawyer, right?"

"Only for the guardianship issue. I wanted to go through the financial end of things, too, to examine her other arrangements, to be sure everything dovetailed nicely, but it was all so rushed she left before we could get to that. The only thing she told me was that her will provisioned the house to Aaron and a trust for Gracie's care. She promised to come back, but…" He sighed. "You know why that didn't happen."

The wheels in Jude's head were turning. "What made her suddenly decide to spell out the guardianship?"

"Great question for which I have no answer." Dan hesitated. "Because I feel involved in the welfare of this child, I would like to delve deeper into the situation. Talk to her other lawyer, with your permission. His name is Bernie Youngblood, out of Las Vegas."

"No harm in one colleague talking to another. The sheriff's department will be all over that, too." And Jude intended to be very involved himself, if Detweiler would allow it. Sure, he'd dated Felicia, and perhaps that hinted at a conflict of interest, but they weren't a couple anymore and wouldn't be again. He was merely a friend helping out. He sneaked a look at her, noting the tear in the knee of her jeans, recalling his exploding pulse as he tried to keep her from being crushed.

A friend, he mentally reiterated. He could feel the concern radiating off her, though she remained silent. Idly he wondered if the scrape on her elbow and knee stung. His own knee was throbbing, and he suspected he'd strained a back muscle with his antics. Small price to pay. Felicia was unharmed, barely. And his sister and Dan were unscathed as well.

Dan nodded. "I'll stay out of law enforcement's way."

Nora smiled. "Dan's excellent at handling awkward situations. Seth said he's helped out at the ranch with all kinds of incomprehensible legalese."

"Thank you," Dan said. "I've encountered plenty of it in my day."

Jude finally spoke up, unable to wait a moment longer. "Dan, who did Keira name as Gracie's guardian?"

The air in the room seemed to thicken. Felicia leaned forward and waited.

Dan cocked his head at her. "You, Felicia," he said. "Keira named you."

FIVE

Time tumbled along in a slow-motion mish-mash. The social worker arrived, a woman named Carol. Vera offered Felicia a cup of hot tea, and Stretch even came and slopped his tongue along the side of her face, but it felt like it was all happening to someone else. She experienced alternating waves of terror and disbelief as Jude spoke with the social worker and Sheriff Fox, the officer assigned by Detweiler. Dan's voice seemed to come from a long way off as he repeated his story for the two. It came back to the same shocking phrase.

You, Felicia. Keira named you.

Me? Gracie's guardian? She felt a squeeze on her shoulder and realized Nora was standing at her side.

"You okay, hon?"

"I'm not really sure."

"This is one of those life bombshells, huh?"

Bombshell didn't begin to describe it. She'd been assigned to raise a child she didn't even know? "I… This is really sudden."

Nora nodded. "I know it's not the same, but for a time our cousin Willow was suddenly responsible for two kids, Tony's niece and nephew. She'd never even babysat as a teen, really. No kid skills. Talk about a mental tsunami."

"How did she manage?"

"I asked her that, too. She said not well at times, but God gave her just enough for each day. Now she loves them more than she ever thought possible."

But I don't want to be somebody's mother right now. Felicia felt guilty about the thought. If her adoptive mother had had a similar attitude, where would Felicia have wound up? But wasn't six months in the hospital and the near-death accidents she'd experienced in the last two days enough? How was she supposed to assimilate this shock, too? She was still reeling when the social worker stood and offered a gentle smile. Nora eased away to give them privacy.

"Miss Tennison, I realize the issue of guardianship wasn't discussed with you beforehand and it's a shock, but let me reassure you it's not set in stone."

Dan had said something similar, but it hadn't penetrated her mental fog. "What do you mean?"

"The issue remains in limbo until a judge rules on the matter. The court will arrange a DNA test as well. I also want you to understand that you are not obligated to accept the guardianship, just because Ms. Silvio drew up the codicil naming you."

Not obligated. She held on to the words like life preservers. A DNA test…nothing set in stone. Felicia tried to process. "So, what you're saying is I'm not really her guardian unless I accept and the judge makes a ruling?"

Carol nodded. "As I said, we know what Keira wanted, but she should have explained it all to you beforehand, discussed it in depth, asked if you were open to the idea. You can absolutely decline. Perhaps there are other relatives or friends willing to step in."

Her heart seized on the thought. She could say no. The little paper doll with a torn pink paper dress caught her attention. "But what will happen to Gracie while it's all being decided?"

The social worker pushed the glasses up her nose. "That's what I wanted to talk to you about. Vera is no longer willing to provide care. Since we know Keira's intentions, Gracie could be placed with you on a temporary basis until the court date is set and other possible kin are contacted. That's liable to take a bit of time due to Mr. Mattingly's expressed intention to adopt Gracie."

Aaron had made it clear. He wanted Gracie. And Keira didn't want him to have her. "And if I don't take her? She won't be living with him, will she?"

"No. We would arrange a foster placement."

Felicia felt dizzy. It was all coming at her so fast. While the courts looked for family, there was still a child whose situation depended on Felicia's decision. She wished the social worker would leave her alone to process her whirling thoughts, but instead she stood there watching, waiting.

"I don't know what to say."

"I understand. I need to talk to Gracie now," Carol said. "Would you like to be there with me and Vera when I tell her?"

"Tell her what?" Felicia managed.

Her expression was tender. "That her mother is deceased."

Felicia gasped. "I thought she might already know."

"Vera wasn't comfortable telling her. She put it off until I arrived."

Felicia's head swam. Jude was suddenly at her side.

"Deep breath." He stroked her forearm. "You don't have to do this if it's too much."

Don't have to... She didn't have to be present when Gracie's world collapsed. Why should she? They were strangers. The whole thing was probably some colossal mistake. Their dimples and similar surgery didn't prove they were sisters. She clutched at his calloused hands, willing it all to go away.

Pain contorted her heart. It was all a bad dream. But if it was her sister... Would she let her own kin go into foster care?

Not fair for either of them. Felicia's life could not simply be catapulted into chaos again, when she'd so narrowly survived the last tsunami. How could God want so much from her?

"One minute," she heard Jude say, and he guided her outside onto the porch. The air was hot now, scalding her skin. He embraced her, and though her brain wanted to pull away, she was simply too overwhelmed to do anything but put her forehead on Jude's wide chest.

He held her, his cheek on top of her head, and she tried to focus on the steady beating of his heart. "Just breathe, Fee."

The nickname he'd used when they were together… She tried, but her lungs fought against her. "I can't do this… I don't *want* to do this."

"And you don't have to. You're not responsible for a kid you never met before."

But her gut told her something much different. What was she doing here, hiding her face in Jude's chest? Jude, the man who'd walked away from her weeks before? She didn't need Jude to tell her what was right. Her conscience was already screaming it, no matter how much she didn't want to listen. Cheeks flaming, she pulled away so fast she almost lost her balance. "I should be with her, at least while they tell her about her mom. I mean, if I'm her sister…"

"We don't know that."

She met his eyes then. They shone with concern, but also with that objective cop thing he had, the way of separating logic from emotion. The facts were unclear. But facts or no facts, the child needed someone while she got the worst news of her short life. Felicia took a steadying breath. "Even if we're not related, I need to be there."

"You don't have to be the one to jump in and rescue her."

Anger flashed bright and stoked her determination. "Because it will be messy? Because I'm afraid?"

He blinked as she continued.

"Maybe I don't have it in me to step up to the guardian plate, but God's going to give me the courage to at least stand by that child while her heart is torn in two."

She could not read his expression.

After a moment, he nodded. "I'll stay outside the door. In case you need…anything."

I won't, she wanted to say, *not from you,* but she was steeped in such a wash of uncertainty, she didn't know if she could stand up to it. With every shred of courage she possessed, she silently prayed and walked back into the house.

The social worker nodded to Jude, who stood at the doorway with Felicia and Vera. Gracie sat on her bed along with the sprawling Stretch, who mouthed a green rope toy. Vera sighed, speaking softly. "Dog practically takes up her whole bed. Keira brought him home shortly after her first husband, Luca, was killed in a hit-and-run. I don't think Keira figured on how huge he was going to get, but he and Gracie took to each other immediately." Vera sniffed. "Aaron couldn't stand the dog. Said he was messy and expensive, but Keira refused to get rid of him."

They watched for a moment until Vera patted Felicia on the back in an unexpected display of emotion. "This is too much. I'll be in the kitchen if you need me."

Jude stepped aside as Felicia entered with the social worker.

Gracie put her pile of crayons in color order in the small cardboard box. The greens and yellows, then the blues and pinks, reds, and finally the neutral colors. Carol and Felicia sat on two card chairs Vera must have fetched.

He knew he didn't add much value to the situation, but he figured he could call for more resources if needed. Felicia talked quietly to Gracie, and he marveled again at her decision to be there. He wasn't sure he would have made the same choice, roles reversed.

Because it will be messy?

Her taunt banged painfully through his insides, like a shutter left open in a windstorm. She was wrong. He hadn't left her because of possible messy complications. He'd done so because it was the best thing for both of them. It had been sheer foolishness on his part to allow his feelings to hinder his good sense in the first place. He had concrete evidence. His own father had betrayed them with one young woman after another before he'd finally left. Dad's decisions had wrecked his mom and driven a wedge between Jude and his sister, Nora, until recently. His own father disgusted him, and he'd resolved never to be an older man trying to hold on to his youth by dating someone younger.

Yet he had, hadn't he? Let their relationship grow for three months knowing full well that Felicia was thirteen years his junior? He was a teenager when she was born, for goodness' sake. At first he'd told himself he'd been merely offering support, visiting her at the hospital, cheering her on through physical therapy, helping her adjust upon her release. Simple friendship, until he'd turned around and found he was falling for her.

There was one moment that convicted him, tore through the tissue-paper lies he'd told himself. It was etched into his mind the day he'd visited her at his cousin Levi's Rocking Horse Ranch, where she was helping Nora take care of Bubbles and her new foal, Pinky. Felicia had been treating Pinky to an ear rub when Bubbles bonked into her from behind and stole the banana she'd put into her back pocket.

Felicia laughed so loud and long that her cheeks went all pink and tears streamed down her face. Jude had laughed, too, equally loud and long, until he'd realized how much her laughter set his own soul flying.

Hard stop right there. Soon after, he'd mumbled through a lame series of "you're a great friend" and "I'm not quality relationship material" excuses until she'd faced him, mouth trembling.

"I get it, Jude. You don't want to be in a relationship with me. Message received."

He blinked back to the present as the social worker spoke to Gracie. "This is Felicia. Your mother wanted you to meet her."

Felicia smiled at Gracie and retrieved a crayon before it rolled off the bed. "You had a heart surgery. I did, too, when I was six." She pulled the neck of her shirt down a few inches to reveal a scar.

Gracie looked curiously at Felicia, but didn't reply, fingering Stretch's floppy ear.

Jude's pulse pounded as Carol delivered the news.

Gracie's face paled and she ducked her chin to her chest. Her tiny sobs knifed through him. Stretch instantly moved closer, sniffing and licking her.

A quiet conversation ensued. Vera poked her head out from the kitchen, her own expression stricken. He tried to look reassuring, but the child's quiet sobbing was the saddest sound he'd ever heard. The cries subsided after a while, along with the dog's distressed whines.

Gracie sat silently. The social worker gently introduced the subject of Vera. "She's not feeling well, and she needs to take care of herself for a while."

Again, the child said nothing at first. "Where are we gonna go?" Her faint whisper made them all jerk a look at her.

"What did you say, Gracie?" the social worker said.

"If Miss Vera doesn't want us to stay here, where are me and Stretch gonna go?"

"I…" Felicia said, interrupting the social worker's answer. He heard Felicia's gulp. "If you want, you can stay with me for a while. Stretch, too."

"Or I can find you another home with a family that will take care of you. You won't be left alone. I promise," Carol said.

Jude realized he was holding his breath.

Gracie buried her head in Stretch's neck, and Jude thought she'd decided not to answer until she looked straight at Felicia, her face swollen from crying. "Okay. We'll go with you."

Felicia explained they'd be staying in Furnace Falls in her mother's house. Jude remembered that the property backed onto an open gully, which would be covered with brush gone dry from a long, brutal summer. Plenty of hiding places, he thought grimly. He didn't know if Aaron was the one who had dropped the rock from the overpass or put the spike strip in the road, but someone wanted to hurt Felicia. He tuned out the conversation.

If the perpetrator tried to repeat the performance, Gracie might be a target, too. He opened his mouth to speak and then closed it.

Gracie was Felicia's business, and that was more than enough for her to tackle.

Their safety was his.

Like it or not, Felicia had just earned herself a Duke protector.

SIX

Felicia helped Gracie into Jude's car, and Stretch lay out across the little girl's lap. Gracie hadn't said much, just allowed Felicia and the social worker to pack a bag for her. Stretch, on the other hand, was vibrating with excitement at the prospect of an adventure. Jude had contacted his cousin Austin about more pet supplies since Austin owned four dogs and bought everything in bulk.

"I'll do some research," Dan said as the tow truck hoisted his ruined Mercedes. Felicia wasn't sure if he meant to dig into the particulars of Keira's trust arrangements or the possibility of other kin who might provide a good home for Gracie. At the moment, Felicia was so frazzled she couldn't give it much consideration. The terrifying thought kept running through her nerve pathways. She was completely responsible for a traumatized child.

Jude was quiet, unsmiling, his gaze often drifting to the side mirror.

Looking for any more threats, she realized. That was another frightening truth, but she pushed it to the fringes of her consciousness by trying to focus on a to-do list. Food, they'd need that. And clean sheets on the bed. A night-light? Had her mother kept any storybooks appropriate for a six-year-old?

Jude pulled up the circular drive to the house. There was still a blackened mark on the cement from the car bomb that had almost killed her. She refused to look at it as she pulled the keys from her pocket. "Here we are, Gracie. There's a nice backyard where you and Stretch can play when it's cooler."

Late-afternoon shadows cloaked the small structure as Jude carried Gracie's things inside. Stretch set to work scrambling off to reconnoiter, but he would return every few moments to observe his young charge. Felicia showed her to the tiny guest room and unloaded some meager belongings into the scratched chest of drawers.

"Deputy Stretch is on duty," Jude said with a chuckle when she joined him in the kitchen while he was checking the window locks.

"I've got Gracie set up in the spare room.

There's a bed barely big enough for her and Stretch. I'll, uh, get some toys or something."

"Nora's waiting for your list, and she also said Beckett and Laney are sending over dinner from the Hotsprings. Beckett insisted you're on paid vacation until you get things settled and not to worry."

Felicia bit her lip. "That is so kind of them."

He shrugged. "They both remember how close they came to losing each other, and they appreciate all your work at the hotel. Laney in particular, since Baby Muffin's eighteen months now and keeping her hopping." He caught her raised brow. "They finally decided on Fiona as a name, but the nickname seems to have stuck." He paused. "Anyway, I'll stay until you're settled."

"No need." She started when there was a knock at the door. After a peek out the window, he admitted Detweiler.

"I understand from Fox that you're taking Gracie in," she said to Felicia.

"Temporarily."

"Is that wise? If you are a target of some sort?"

Felicia spread her hands. "I don't know, but I think it's what's best for Gracie right now since her world has fallen apart."

Stretch zoomed close and sniffed at Detweiler's boots before scampering back to the bedroom. Her eyes went wide. "That thing's massive."

"Yes, ma'am. What have you got?" Jude's words made Felicia's stomach tighten. Of course Detweiler hadn't come for a social visit.

"Aaron Mattingly says he was at home working on funeral arrangements at the time the booby trap was laid in the road at Vera's house."

"Can anyone corroborate?"

"No, but we have no eyewitnesses to put him at the scene, either, so that's a standoff." She looked hesitant, as if she didn't want to discuss police matters in front of Felicia. Jude, too, shot an uncertain glance her way.

Her nerves went steely. If they thought she was going to be talked around as if she wasn't strong or grown-up enough to hear the facts, they had another think coming. Especially Jude. She lifted her chin. "Okay. So what are the next steps?"

"I'm working the motive angle," Detweiler said.

"Following the money, like Jude says?"

Detweiler raised a brow. "Yes, as a matter of fact. I talked to Bernie Youngblood, Keira's original lawyer, via a video chat. He'd been on a golfing trip and didn't get Keira's message until it was too late, which is why he figures she went to Dan Wheatly. He's providing copies of her estate, and at the surface, it's pretty normal. Aaron gets the house and contents. The rest of the assets fall into a trust set up for Gracie, which was started with a settlement Luca got for a work-related injury at his trucking company. It's a small chunk of change, twenty thousand dollars. Whatever isn't needed for expenses will be given to Gracie when she's twenty-five. Aaron was the previous executor of that trust, but the codicil transfers that power to you."

Felicia was stuck on the word *expenses*. She hadn't considered until that moment how Gracie's guardianship would be funded. Clothes, food, medical care, college tuition… Her throat tightened. Her work at the Hotsprings and the donkey rescue barely kept her afloat. Another reason to hope there was a more well-off relative waiting in the wings to take over.

"So Aaron's original plan could have been to adopt Gracie and murder Keira to get his hands on the trust," Jude said.

"Shhhh." Felicia pointed a finger in the direction of the hallway.

"Oh, sorry." Jude continued in a quieter tone.

"Twenty thousand doesn't seem like enough of a motive, but we've encountered plenty of killers who would do it for less. So when Aaron discovered that Felicia's been appointed guardian, he decided to eliminate her?"

Detweiler nodded. "Possibly, but I don't understand that as a motive. He'd hear from his lawyer that Felicia's codicil superseded any unfinished adoption proceedings he'd started. It's not like things would change if he disposed of Felicia. He wouldn't suddenly be granted custody when Keira clearly didn't want that."

"Could be he thinks if I'm gone the court would have no choice but to award him custody and hence the trust," Felicia said.

"That's a long shot, isn't it?" Detweiler said. "And it could take time to decide the matter legally. Right now, he gets the house, period. And if you were out of the picture, Felicia, the executor job defaults to Youngblood, not Aaron. I would believe he might have dropped the rock to prevent Keira from meeting with you if he'd found out about that somehow, but once he'd been told she'd met with a lawyer to change her will, why set up the spike strip?"

"Revenge." Felicia forced out the word. "He had a plan worked out, and Keira changed it all with that codicil. If I became the guardian, I'd be the person who's getting everything he feels he's entitled to." Cold took hold of her insides, even though the house was stuffy.

Detweiler was watching her closely. "It's a lot to risk for revenge."

Felicia faced her full-on. "I spent six months in a hospital bed courtesy of a man who thought I was standing in the way of what he deserved."

"That's not going to happen again," Jude said.

Oh, how she wanted to believe him, but she knew his determination wasn't a guarantee. Nothing was, outside of salvation.

"But to be sure you're safe, it would be easier if you weren't..." Detweiler said.

"Taking care of Gracie?"

They both looked at her.

"Believe me, I'd rest easier handing this whole situation over to someone else, but the fact of the matter is, that probably means a foster-care placement with someone she's never met. I'm not the greatest choice maybe, but at least she can stay in the same area with her dog."

"Felicia..." Jude started.

"For some reason her mother picked me," she blurted. "I can at least stick it out until they find a relative." Tears threatened suddenly. "I'm going to go ask Gracie if she needs a snack."

She escaped down the hallway before they could see her doubt. She believed she was doing the right thing for Gracie…but with Aaron out for blood, would she be strong enough to ensure the child's safety?

Detweiler pursed her lips. They stood for a moment in silence before she spoke again. "If Aaron hates her that much that he's tried to kill her twice…" She let the words trail off.

"Not gonna happen." Jude spoke before he could think the better of it.

Detweiler looked at him oddly. "In case you missed it, I've assigned Fox to this case."

Fox, the last person he wanted to share anything with. "Furnace Falls is my town."

"No." She drew out the word. "Furnace Falls is your *assignment*, at the moment. And you've got plenty to do without being involved here."

"I've got a good department to pick up the slack. It's no problem for me to provide additional protection while Fox handles the primary investigation."

She shook her head. "You're too close. Fox will check in on them."

"She needs more than a check-in." *Especially from Fox.*

"Sheriff Duke," Detweiler said, "are you telling me how to do my job?"

Are you telling me how to do mine? He breathed away the belligerence collecting in his belly. "No, ma'am, I'm simply saying I am a better fit to oversee this case than Fox."

"Be careful, Jude. You're letting your feelings cloud your judgment in more ways than one."

He started to reply, when she held up a finger. "Fox is the point person." She tacked on, "Whether you like him or not."

Like him? Jude could hardly stand being in the same room with the older man who was his father's longtime buddy. Fox had been a mentor when Jude was a wet-behind-the-ears recruit. In those long ten months together, Fox had never seen fit to tell him his father was busily gambling away their mother's money, though he full well knew it. The more distance between Jude and Fox, the better.

He bit back a retort, knowing he had to tread carefully. Not the time to exercise his stubborn streak. *"Don't say the first thing that pops into your head,"* his sister, Nora, used to tell him. *"Try for the second or third."*

"What do you have on Keira's death?"

"Forensics are in progress, but that's gonna

be a while. Witnesses saw her leaving the coffee shop like you said. Aaron claims she returned to their Las Vegas home and napped, they had dinner as usual and she began to act paranoid, saying he was having an affair, wanting to steal Gracie from her, that kind of thing. He said she left around five, and he went to find her a couple of hours later. Neighbors weren't home, so we have no corroboration of any of that. Aaron's prints were all over her car, but they're married, so you'd expect that."

"Aaron might have been tracking her. She lost him and went to meet with Dan, but he found her again afterward and killed her. What about the first husband's death? Could Aaron have been involved in that?"

"We're pulling those files. Luca died from a hit-and-run. No arrest was made."

"It was Aaron on that overpass. I can feel it. He's behind the spike-strip thing, too."

"I'll pass along your thoughts to Fox." She turned to go. "Jude, I mean it. I don't want you muddying up the waters. If there's a case to be made against Aaron, it isn't yours, no matter how fond you are of Felicia."

He realized at that moment that Felicia had just set foot on the kitchen linoleum.

Her face burned rosy as a desert sunrise. He

could feel the heat in his own cheeks. *Thanks a lot, Detweiler.*

Detweiler looked at Felicia. "How's Gracie?" she asked, not unkindly.

"Bewildered, I think. About like I am."

Detweiler nodded. "She's my granddaughter's age. Can't imagine how she's feeling. Let me know if there's anything we can do to assist in addition to the social worker."

Felicia nodded and Detweiler said goodbye.

When the door closed behind the head sheriff, Jude stood uncertainly, wondering what in the world he should be doing or saying. Felicia filled a bowl of water and put it on a mat for the dog. "I...get the sense your boss still doesn't want you involved in this situation."

"She's not wild about the idea."

Without making eye contact, she said, "I hope taking me to Vera's didn't get you in trouble."

"A little trouble isn't a problem."

"Thank you for helping me get Gracie. I'll be able to handle things from here."

She was trying to dismiss him, but he was not anywhere near ready to leave. "Sure," he said, going for nonchalance. "Just helping you move Gracie in. And waiting for dinner. I'm starving. You don't mind if I eat here with you two, do you? All I've had today is three cups of coffee."

She fiddled with her shirt, still not meeting his eyes. She'd stood right up to Detweiler and him earlier, but now she looked tentative. He was sorry he'd made her feel that way, but not sorry enough to depart just yet.

"Okay," she said, after a long pause. "It might help to have someone else around to keep the conversation going with Gracie."

Perfect. It would give him time to stroll outside along the gully and check security there. If Fox was going to be stopping by, he'd make sure the man knew all the possible weak points.

Not involved. Darkness began to creep over the house, and he thought of Felicia and Gracie, alone and vulnerable. He was simply a concerned party.

Very concerned.

SEVEN

Felicia wasn't sure if her constant checking on Gracie was helpful or smothering. Then again, it might simply be a way to avoid other uncomfortable scenarios. The fact was she didn't want to be sitting in the kitchen making conversation with Jude. Their chats had flowed so easily when they were dating seriously. *It was only serious in your mind*, she reminded herself bitterly. He'd had no problem walking away, had he?

Annoyed with herself for allowing her thoughts to circle back to Jude, she again checked her phone. Her uncle had still not returned her call, and there was no progress update from the police or social worker. What had she expected? That they'd immediately arrest Aaron? The social worker would locate a loving aunt yearning to take Gracie?

Though she longed to place a call to Greece, Felicia could not fathom how to explain her current status without upsetting her mother. Wandering from the hallway to the living room and back again, she was caught in a kind of frustrating limbo.

Jude took Stretch outside for a potty break while Felicia showed Gracie the bathroom and offered her the best of the guest towels. Stretch lapped up a bowl of water when he returned, sloshing much of it on the floor before he returned to Gracie in the bedroom.

The girl still had not spoken more than a couple of sentences. Was that normal? *Nothing about this is normal*. Should she press? Uncertain, she dried up the water as the doorbell rang.

Jude's cousin Willow Duke and a handsome, dark-haired man stood on the stoop, arms full of grocery bags, a little boy and girl with them.

"Hiya," Willow said. "Beckett and Laney sent us. This is Tony, and his nephew Carter and niece Bee. We're watching them while Tony's brother's out of town."

"I brought my coloring books." Carter sported a shock of hair that stood up on top of his head like a flag. "I got them for my birthday. I turned six last week."

"Me, too," Bee piped up.

"Twins," Tony said, "but Bee's the pint-sized

version. We thought maybe Gracie could use some company her own age."

"That's very sweet of you."

"Yeah, an excellent idea." Jude took a bag from Tony. "And I smell food, so that's a double bonus."

There was a clatter of toenails on the hardwood. Bee shrieked and Tony stepped in front of her protectively as Stretch galloped over to sniff them, Gracie following behind her giant dog.

"Lion," Bee squealed.

Willow patted her head. "No, just a really big dog. Remember I told you Gracie has Stretch? He's friendly, super chill."

As if to prove the point, Stretch collapsed onto the floor on his back, legs bicycling the air until Willow and then Carter scratched his tummy. All three kids chortled, and Felicia laughed right along with them, a blessed release. She couldn't remember the last time she'd let loose with a chuckle. Before she could escort the children to Gracie's room, the doorbell rang again.

A tall, blond man greeted her, an enormous bag of dog chow in his arms and a sturdy leash draped around his neck. She'd met him only a few times, Jude's cousin Austin Duke. "Greetings. I heard you needed pet assistance, so I was dispatched."

"You're a lifesaver." She had almost gotten the door shut when another couple appeared on the doorstep. Nora and her new husband, Seth. "We're the meals on wheels," he said with a wink. Felicia gave Seth an extra-tight hug. The man had saved her life with his combat medic skills after the explosion. She'd always be grateful and happy that Seth had come into their lives and married her best friend.

Felicia felt an additional swell of gratitude as the parade of Jude's kin settled in. The Duke clan was an army of big hearts and helping hands. While she set the table, Nora opened the dinner containers, releasing a mouthwatering aroma, while Willow took charge of introducing the children to each other.

Tony, Seth and Jude began to talk quietly in the corner. Battle plans? That made her nervous, since Jude was supposed to be removing himself from her situation. *My battle isn't yours.* Tension coiled inside her as she took in Jude's handsome profile. She'd never seen him as an older man, just a person she'd foolishly let herself care for. Maybe she'd been emotionally off-balance from her extended hospital stay.

Whatever. Quit going back there. The most

important thing for her to do was to handle her situation and keep their entanglement where it belonged, buried deep. She marched down the hall and peeked into Gracie's room. Stretch had been let out for a romp in the shallow gully, and Willow sat on a chair in the corner, observing.

Bee was busily dressing a doll she must have brought in her kid-sized backpack, oblivious to the other two children, who were occupied with coloring. Carter labored on a picture of airplanes, while Gracie sketched on a piece of plain paper. Felicia saw she was creating a picture of Stretch in all his slobbery glory. The sight of Gracie there, engaged in something as mundane and sweet as an impromptu playdate with other children she'd only just met, made Felicia's eyes swim. Moments of normalcy. In the hospital, she'd clung to those. A phone call from a friend. A walk, even if it was only a few feet. Wearing pajamas brought from home instead of a standard-issue gown. God had given her enough of those moments to keep her going. *If that's what I can give Gracie, Lord, please help me do it.*

Willow sniffed. "Smells like dinner. Who's hungry?"

"Meeeeee," Bee sang out, which made Gracie smile. *There's the dimple.* Family trait or coincidence? She thought of Keira. Her mother? Their mother? No relation at all?

Willow snapped her out of her reverie. "You coming?"

Felicia realized the children had already filed out the door and into the bathroom to wash their hands. When they squeezed around the dining room table, Felicia said grace. She was pleased that Gracie folded her hands quickly, obviously used to praying before a meal. Another commonality.

With the conversation bubbling all around, Felicia ate and listened, noting that Gracie consumed at least a few bites of the cheesy lasagna. She resisted the urge to encourage the child to finish her milk. *You're not her mother, remember? And she's six years old, not a baby.* Her permanent guardian would be responsible for enforcing mom-type rules. The children returned to the bedroom to finish coloring, Stretch at their heels.

Her phone buzzed with a text, and she stepped away from the table to check her screen, returning quickly.

"Everything all right?" Jude asked.

"Vera just reminded me that Gracie has a doctor's appointment in town tomorrow morning, but my car's still in the shop."

"I'll take you," three voices said at once.

Tony, Seth and Jude had all offered at precisely the same moment. Her heart swelled at the compassion this family had offered her.

"I will take her," Jude said firmly. "It's on my way."

She'd much rather have accepted either of the other two offers, but neither Tony nor Seth argued the point with Jude.

"Um, and we'll have our DNA test done then, too."

Jude's smile was encouraging. "Good. Then everything will be clear, right?"

Would it?

"This is an emotional situation, Jude," Nora said. "It's not like she's having a car engine looked at or something."

Jude jerked a look at his sister. "Oh, well, sure. I only meant that decisions would be easier."

Willow sighed. "Big decisions about children are never easy. Even the little ones. We took care of the kids for three weeks last month while their dad traveled for business, and I spent hours trying to figure out what to feed them. I cooked for days, and they barely ate any of it."

Everyone pitched in to clear the table and start on the dishes. When the sun vanished completely beyond the distant mountains, the Duke family excused themselves.

Nora wrapped an arm around Felicia and kissed her cheek. "I put some teddy bear sheets on the bed. I know she's six and all, but they were pink and cute. And there's a new toothbrush and bubble-mint-flavored toothpaste in the bathroom that Seth says his nephew likes."

Felicia squeezed her back gratefully. "It didn't even occur to me to think about toothpaste flavors. I'm not on top of any of this."

"You're loving one moment at a time. That's all God asks of anyone, right? Call me if you need anything."

Felicia promised. She shut the door after their departure. Stretch was nosing around under the kitchen table to hoover up crumbs, so she set out a bowl of kibble for him. While he wolfed it down, she led Gracie to the bathroom and pointed out the new toothpaste and toothbrush.

"And, um, if you want to take a shower, I can turn on the water for you."

Gracie nodded. "Mommy makes sure it's not too hot."

Mommy. Felicia's heart squeezed as she watched the grief ripple over Gracie's face. She laid a hand gently on the crown of Gracie's head. She didn't know what to say, so she held still. Gracie turned into her arms and sobbed. Felicia embraced her until she was done.

While Gracie wiped her face, Felicia turned on the water and got it adjusted to an acceptable temperature. Gracie stood, clutching the towel.

Did six-year-olds manage their own dressing and undressing? Perhaps she was sore from her recent surgery? The wound was well covered with a waterproof pad, but she hadn't specifically asked a doctor about it. Why hadn't she thought of it before? "Is it all right to get your incision site wet?"

Gracie nodded. "Doc Howley said it's okay to shower now, but no bath."

It hit Felicia like a bolt that she would be the person responsible for gathering information from the doctor the next day.

Gracie watched her as steam began to fill the room.

"Uh, did you need other help? I mean, with undressing or…"

"I can do it." The words were so soft she almost didn't catch them.

"All right. I'll pull the door closed except for a crack so I can hear you if you call. Okay?"

Gracie nodded, but before Felicia exited, Stretch plowed into the small bathroom, banging the door into the wall.

"Stretch, you have to wait in the hall," Felicia said. "There's no room in here."

The dog lashed his tail with such eagerness he knocked Gracie's pajamas off the countertop.

Felicia picked them up.

"Sit," Gracie said.

The dog promptly dropped to the tile. It was more of a sprawl than a sit, and Felicia was forced back against the wall since he took up almost all the available floor space.

"He can stay here while I shower," Gracie said.

Stretch busied himself licking the baseboards. Figuring it couldn't hurt to let the massive dog wait it out in the bathroom, Felicia nodded and returned to the kitchen to find Jude scrubbing the lasagna pan. Why hadn't he left with the others?

"You don't have to do that."

"No bother." Water and suds splashed around his sinewy forearms.

She picked up a towel and dried a dish, clunking it against the counter in her agitation. Weariness eroded her filter. "Jude, what's going on here?"

"I'm scrubbing a dish that someone should have spritzed with cooking spray, I might add. Would've saved me a lot of elbow grease."

"No, I mean, why are you still here?" When he started to answer, she shook her head. "And I'm not talking about you washing dishes."

He pulled the glassware from the soapy water, rinsed it and set it on the drainer before drying his hands. "I'm concerned that you aren't safe."

"That part I understand, but your boss made it clear you're not supposed to interfere in this case. Someone else was assigned."

"Washing dishes isn't interference in a police investigation, is it?"

"You're intentionally being obtuse."

"Nah, I'm naturally obtuse." For some reason, his smile drained her ire away.

"I'm too tired for joking. I'm not your job. I'm not your girlfriend. You don't owe me anything."

"That's not it, but while we're on the subject, I do owe you an apology for the way I left things."

Things, as if she was a fishing rod or rifle abandoned without proper care. "We don't need to go into that. I just want it clear that you shouldn't take care of me out of guilt."

"It's not…" He cleared his throat. Probably he'd realized that was exactly why he was still there in her mother's tiny home. He snagged her gaze with his navy blue one. "You live in Furnace Falls. I'm the acting chief of this town, alongside my sheriff duties. That makes you my responsibility, no matter what Detweiler says."

A responsibility. That was worse than a thing.

"I appreciate your sense of duty," she said stiffly, "but I don't want private protection from the chief, and since Detweiler is your boss, you should follow her orders."

His mouth tightened. "Do you want me to go?"

She tipped her chin up and forced it out. "Yes."

"That hurts." He smiled, but his eyes didn't.

"I'm sorry it does." *Just like when you told me goodbye.* "I'm not a special case, and I'm sure Sheriff Fox can handle my protection and Gracie's."

"There might be more attacks."

"But Aaron knows he's being watched now. Detweiler and Fox have interviewed him. That should be a deterrent."

"Wasn't for the guy who hurt you before."

Her blood went hot with anger. "Don't you dare, Jude. Don't you ever use what happened to me before to make me live in fear. I won't allow it. Not from myself and not from you."

He grimaced. "I'm sorry, Felicia. I shouldn't have said that, but..."

She raised a finger. "Genuine apologies don't have a *but* in them."

He opened his mouth, then closed it and nodded. "You're right. As soon as Fox checks in, I'll go. He's en route from the station, so it won't be long. Until then, I'll dry dishes and keep out of your way." He held out his palm. "Do we have a bargain?"

She took his hand and shook it, finding the strong fingers gentle.

"I am sorry." He brought her hand to his mouth for a kiss. "I don't ever want to hurt you."

Her heart pounded at the feel of his lips on her hand. Then she pulled away, slightly breathless. "Okay." He would leave soon, like she wanted. Why did she feel even more uncertain now that he'd agreed? She was still scared about Aaron and tending to Gracie; the upcoming DNA test worried her, and the hurt from Jude's betrayal blew through her soul as strongly as it ever had.

Without a word, she went to tackle bedtime rituals for a child she barely knew.

EIGHT

A half hour later, Jude was standing with arms folded in the kitchen, facing his fellow sheriff. Fox scrubbed a palm over his bald head as he listened to Jude's report. Shadows under his eyes gave the impression he'd had a long and tiring day. They all had. Some common ground, at least.

"Look, Jude, I'm fairly confident we sent Aaron Mattingly a message that he's under scrutiny. He's had his shot at revenge if that's what it was, but he's a smart guy. I think he'll wise up and quit causing trouble now."

"That's not a risk we should take. Felicia needs protection, especially now that she's caring for Gracie."

"I understand. I'm not suggesting she's on her own. I'll be driving by this place every four hours."

"That's not good enough."

One grizzled brow crawled up Fox's forehead. "That's what we would offer any citizen of this community, wouldn't we?"

She's not any citizen. "This is a special case. There's a child at risk here, too, a kid who's suffered a significant trauma already."

"I understand that. I'll make sure Felicia has my direct cell number in case she feels at all nervous about anything."

"I'm not satisfied."

Now Fox's eyes narrowed. "With the arrangements or the fact that I'm in charge?"

Jude had to will himself not to grind his teeth together. "No secret that we don't get along."

"The whole grudge is ridiculous. When you gonna let the past be the past? That was twenty years ago, Jude."

"Not ridiculous to me. My mother never recovered financially, thanks to your good buddy, my father. Or maybe you forgot that?"

"That's your beef with your dad, not with me."

"We are colleagues. Brothers in blue. All those years ago you knew my mom was being bled dry, and you didn't tell me. Cops are supposed to have each other's backs, last I checked."

"Yeah, but they aren't supposed to stick their

noses into family business. I'm not a marriage counselor. Live and let live, that's my motto."

Easy to say when it wasn't your mother. Jude glared at him. "It says something about the character of a man who doesn't step in when he should."

Fox's smile vanished and he shuffled closer. "Maybe it says more when a man steps into something when he shouldn't. Is all this blustering on your part really because you don't like me?"

"Are you suggesting another reason?"

Fox shrugged. "Heard you were dating Felicia and you dumped her a couple of weeks back. Trying to mend some fences? Maybe looking to rekindle a romance again?"

Jude could hardly contain his anger. "Listen to me..." he snarled.

Felicia walked in. He eased back, forcing a calmer tone and going for a smile. "Did you get Gracie to sleep?"

"She's not sleeping, but with Stretch draped across her legs, she won't feel scared. We read a story together." He saw the emotion rippling under her calm facade. She was terrified, and not just of Aaron's threats. Her whole life had done a 180, and the fallout was still landing. Anybody should know that, Fox included. The danger wasn't over, and it was another stressor on a woman already burdened.

Fox introduced himself and handed Felicia a card. He discussed his check-in plan and assured her he'd examined the grounds. "Doors and windows are all secure and yard's clear. Call me anytime. I'll alert you if we discover anything about Aaron or whoever else is involved in this situation." His radio squawked and he listened to Dispatch. "Overturned tractor trailer. Gotta roll, but I'll drive by again in a few hours, okay?"

Felicia nodded and thanked him.

Fox stared hard at Jude from the doorway. "I imagine you'll be gone when I drive by, Sheriff Duke. Safe travels."

He didn't dare say a word. Fox left, and he attacked the remaining dishes with such force he cracked one.

Felicia took it from him and set it aside. "Why don't you like him?"

Jude clammed up, his go-to mode. "Doesn't matter."

"It does matter." She waited, arms crossed. "I'm not a child, and I have a right to know what kind of person is supposed to be protecting me."

I should be that person. What was going on

with his brain? He didn't want to tell her, nor anyone, why he despised Fox. Matter of fact, he hadn't discussed his feelings about what had happened with anyone. "As a cop, he's competent. It's personal between us." He hoped to stop there but her silence told him that plan was out the window. "He's my dad's buddy. He knew Dear Old Dad was gambling away my mom's savings, and he didn't tell me."

Her eyes went round. "Oh. I can see why that would be upsetting."

"Yeah, well, I know you're going to say it's got nothing to do with him doing his job and I'm letting my anger get in the way of my professionalism." He threw down the towel. "I get it and you're probably right. I'll head out now." He'd drive away, bring his feelings under control before he blabbed anything else. Figure out next steps.

She stopped him with a hand on his arm. That touch was light as a sifting of sand, but it seemed to envelop him, anchor him. "Actually," she said, the hazel of her eyes almost gold in the dim light, "I was going to say thank you."

"For what?"

"Respecting me enough to tell me the truth."

"I…uh… You're welcome." For the life of him, he couldn't quite figure out how his temper tantrum about Fox deserved thanks, but he'd take it.

She moved her hand away. "I'll call Fox if anything is out of the ordinary."

Jude sighed. "All right. How about I take Stretch out back one more time so he doesn't wake you up in the night?" He liked the idea that she wouldn't need to unlock the slider until the following morning.

"I'd appreciate it. I'll go tell Gracie."

Jude followed her down the hallway and peered into the tiny bedroom. Gracie was rolled into a ball with Stretch beside her on the bed, one gangly leg atop hers. She was sound asleep, the covers pulled up almost over her nose. *So small. So young to have lost everything.*

"Come here, Stretch," Felicia whispered.

It took coaxing and a treat bribe, but Stretch finally acquiesced and Jude led him away from the bedroom. It was disarming walking next to a dog that stood higher than his waist. Stretch was the perfect name.

He slid open the glass door, and the dog trotted outside as the phone in the living room rang. A landline, how novel.

Felicia picked it up. "Hello?" There was a pause of a few seconds. "Hello? Is anyone there?"

Her voice pitched higher with tension. Instinct quivered in Jude's belly. He left Stretch to meander about and joined Felicia.

She frowned, chewing her lip. "Who's calling?"

He gestured for her to hold the phone out so he could hear also. She did and he leaned in, his cheek brushing her temple.

No one spoke—at least, not at first.

A three-second pause, then a hard, raspy whisper, male.

"So easy."

Felicia recoiled, almost dropping the phone. Jude seized the receiver.

"Who is this?" He received only a quiet laugh in response. He started to demand an answer a second time when Stretch began to bark from the yard.

Urgent, intense barking that made Jude run for the door with his hand on his gun. "Lock me out. I'll tell you when it's safe to open up."

He slammed outside, the darkness wrapping around him like a velvet blindfold.

Cold panic surged through Felicia. She realized she was still holding the phone to her ear, now listening to a dial tone. The mysterious caller had hung up. But was he really gone?

What had he meant? *So easy?* But in her heart she already knew the answer. It would be an uncomplicated thing to get to her, or Gracie. Perhaps the caller was in the backyard right now, watching. Her skin felt clammy and dread clawed at her from inside. Could he be out there? Aaron or whoever had tried to kill her near the overpass?

A more insistent urge pulled at her. *Get to Gracie. Protect her.* Felicia ran down the hall. Gracie was still asleep, so she hurried to the window. The lock was engaged, safe and secure. She went still, listening. Outside she could no longer hear Stretch barking. Pulling the curtain aside a few inches, she peered out. It was overwhelmingly dark at first, the thumbnail moon screened by a wall of clouds. Then a light crept across the yard, arcing one luminous inch at a time. A flashlight? Was it Jude? The beam crept slowly toward the house, toward the room where she now stood looking out.

So easy.

What if Aaron was out there hiding undiscovered by Jude? Should she call Fox? Or 911? She grabbed her cell phone, fingers ready to dial. Where was Jude? Who was out there? As the minutes ticked by, her anxiety grew.

And then she heard claws scratching on the

sliding door. Heart pounding, she ran back to the living room. Stretch pawed again at the glass, asking to be let in.

But Jude had said he would tell her when she should unlock it. Torn with indecision, she almost screamed as Jude surged into view. Hurriedly she unfastened the slider and flung it open. He came inside right after Stretch and immediately relocked it behind them. "All clear now."

"Now?"

Jude grabbed the house phone and thumbed "recent calls" before he dialed his own cell. His expression was grave as he waited for someone to pick up. "I didn't detect any tracks, but the ground's rocky and dry, so it'd be hard to see. It might have been Stretch barking at a squirrel or raccoon."

She swallowed. "Or it might have been whoever just called."

He nodded. When Fox answered his cell, Jude succinctly reported what had happened.

Stretch edged up close to Felicia, waiting to see if he would be offered a treat. She obliged. "You're a good boy," she told him, rubbing his silky neck after he gulped the biscuit. Stretch was better than any alarm system. He waited a moment to see if there were more treats coming and then lumbered off to Gracie's room.

Felicia saw Jude's mouth tighten into a thin line as he listened to Fox. "It's intimidation—like the rock and the accident at Vera's." He paused, listening. "Copy that." He punched the phone off. "He's starting a trace via the tech people to see if he can pinpoint the source of the call, and he's contacting Las Vegas PD to check Aaron's place right now and see if he's home." He paused. "Gracie okay?"

"Still sleeping."

"Good. No reason she should be scared."

Felicia was scared enough for both of them. All of a sudden, the small house she'd known since she was two years old seemed filled with dark corners. She turned on the lamp.

He touched her shoulder and she almost screamed.

"It's okay," he said.

"How is this okay? I'm a mess and I'm supposed to be strong for Gracie."

He almost smiled. "You are strong."

"Strong people don't freak out over a phone call and a dog barking."

"Extenuating circumstances." He quirked a grin at her. "I freaked out when I found a mouse in my gun safe. Trust me, it wasn't pretty, and if you tell anyone, I'll completely deny it."

She couldn't help herself. She laughed, releasing some of the bottled-up fear. It took the fright down one level. "I'd have paid an entrance fee to see that."

"Like I said, not pretty." He surveyed the living room. "I checked all the windows and doors again while I was out there. No signs of tampering, but to be cautious, I'm going to sleep on the sofa." He didn't look at her.

"Jude…"

He held up his palms. "I know, you're unhappy about it."

"Jude…"

"But it's only for one night, or possibly a couple of hours, until we get an answer back on the source of the phone call."

"I…"

"I won't be a bit of trouble. I'll camp out in this room and you'll hardly know I'm here. You've got that early-morning doctor run, which I'm driving you to anyway, so it would be easier if I stayed."

"Jude." She spoke loudly enough that he finally stopped talking.

"What?" His look said, *You're not going to win this one.* Surprisingly, she found she didn't want to.

She tried to keep the relief from her voice. "I'll get you a blanket."

He closed his mouth. "Okay."

As she fetched a throw and a pillow from the closet, she acknowledged that she was extremely relieved not to be alone those long hours until dawn.

If Aaron was out there, set on revenge, he wouldn't get close, not with Jude there. At least, not for another night. Jude's presence comforted her.

Not comforted, she told herself. Reassured, was all, a temporary help.

When the morning came, she'd have to face her fears by herself.

Exhausted, she crawled into bed and prayed.

NINE

Jude was working on his second cup of coffee when Felicia padded barefoot into the kitchen. Immediately, he fetched a mug and poured her one, adding one packet of sugar, the way she preferred. Why did his brain hold on to such details when his heart had walked away?

"Thank you." She took it and his fingers brushed hers. Her hair was damp, feathered against her troubled brow.

"Sleep any?"

"Not much. My uncle called late and I filled him in. He's horrified and wants us to come stay at the camp."

Jude's mental wheels churned. Would security be better there? Or would she be more exposed? And how would he keep eyes on Felicia and Gracie if they were tucked away with her uncle?

"What about you?" She yawned. "Isn't this supposed to be your day off?"

"The wheels of justice never rest."

"Uh-huh, but the people who turn the wheels do." She eyed his open laptop. "You didn't work all night, did you?"

"Catnapped. Don't tell Stretch." He sat at the table and she joined him. "Fox sent me the intel on Aaron Mattingly."

She perched next to him. "And?"

"He was a coworker of Luca's before Luca died. They met five years ago at Starlight Trucking Company, based out of Las Vegas. They were both drivers, but Aaron was essentially fired after an accident where he rammed his rig into a tree. He was hired back as a night custodian at a fraction of his former salary. He drove a truck in New York before he was hired at Starlight. His first wife was a woman named Eliza. Eliza's mom became sick with cancer, which is why they relocated to this area from the East Coast. Three months after Eliza's mom passed, they divorced and she moved back to New York."

"How did he meet Keira?"

"Company picnic. It was a casual acquaintance until after Luca's death. Then Aaron employed the casserole rule."

"The what?"

"He showed up with a casserole and comfort. That got the ball rolling on their relationship. Aaron told Fox he was a great support to Keira after she was widowed, and their relationship grew from there. Aaron listed all the kudos he felt he was owed for the things he'd done for Gracie over the years—attending tiny-tot classes, ballet recitals, the whole nine yards."

"Is it possible his love for her was genuine? From what Dan said, Keira wasn't a wealthy woman. Maybe Aaron did really have feelings for her and we're being cynical."

"*I'm* being cynical, you mean." Jude smiled over his coffee mug. "Probably. Aaron could actually be a sweet guy, misunderstood, and maybe he really does love Gracie. It's likely he's not behind these attacks." *But that's not what my gut says*, he refrained from adding.

She went silent, stirring her coffee in an endless swirl.

"I couldn't find any tracks outside. Stretch may have been reacting to something completely unrelated. Fox said they couldn't trace the source of the call. The caller used a burner app and deleted the number, so it literally doesn't exist anymore. If we had more probable cause, we could subpoena records from his provider and track call logs, approximate location, et cetera, but we're not in a position to do that at the moment."

She shook her head and he knew what she was thinking. Tentatively, he palmed her hand in his. "Whoever made the call took the easy way out. Threatening from afar is a coward's way. Cowards don't have the guts to hurt people in person." *Most of the time.* It was the same thing Fox said when they'd talked after his early-morning check of the property. Fox was of the opinion the phone call was a crank. Jude had not seen fit to tell his cohort he'd kept watch on the sofa overnight.

She blew out a breath. "Mickey Mouse or plain?"

He blinked. "Huh?"

"I'm making pancakes for Gracie, and I found out she really likes Mickey Mouse, so I'm getting creative. What's your order?"

He laughed, delighted for no particular reason he could identify. "In view of my cowardice toward mice, I'll go with plain."

"Done." She pulled on an apron and tied it around her waist. "And after the doctor appointment, if you can drop me at the garage to pick up Audrey, you won't have to tote us everywhere."

And he wouldn't have a reason to stay at her house, either. It would all be up to Fox, unless he figured out another way to remain involved. He cleared away his computer. Felicia called out, and Gracie and Stretch arrived at the table.

Gracie didn't say anything about the mouse pancake, but Jude thought he saw her smile at her plate. They ate, Jude and Felicia making forced cheerful small talk about weather and animals and Carter and Bee while Stretch crunched away at his dog food. Jude tackled the dishes as Felicia helped Gracie find a sweater. It was going to be way too hot for that, he figured, but maybe it was a comfort thing. Stretch reached his massive head up and, with his teeth, lifted the leash Austin had provided from the hook next to the door. His whip of a tail ricocheted hopefully. "Sorry, boy. You're not invited this time."

Gracie frowned. "The doctor said it's okay to bring Stretch if he doesn't eat the crayons in the waiting room."

"I'm not sure…" Felicia started.

"Mommy let me take him places. Every time." There was a slight hint of hysteria in the words. Gracie's eyes suddenly filled with tears, and she pinched her lips tight together. Stretch shoved his head under her arm, the leash jangling as he licked her.

Something inside Jude melted at Gracie's sadness. "Oh hey, then. If it's okay with Doc, I guess he can sit with me in the waiting room." He sent a panicked look at Felicia for confirmation. She nodded her agreement. "If he starts to go for the crayons, I'll take him outside while you have your checkup. How's that?"

He was immensely relieved that Gracie offered a weak smile. "That's good," she said.

"Ladies," he said, looking at the side table, "has anyone seen my cap?"

Gracie appeared very interested in the linoleum. He raised an eyebrow. "Miss Gracie? Might you know where my baseball cap has gotten to? It says Inyo County Sheriff on it, and I've just broken it in the way I like."

Grimacing, she went to a drawer and pulled out the tattered remains of Jude's hat. "Stretch likes caps. And he can reach 'most anything."

"I'll keep that in mind." He dropped the wreckage into the wastebasket with a sigh.

He was pretty sure Felicia was trying to hold back her laughter as he led them to his car. She buckled Gracie in the back with Stretch, then climbed into the passenger side. He lowered the window to let in some air. It was likely going to hit ninety by lunchtime. Stretch shoved his head out, and his fleshy lips flapped madly in the wind. All three of them laughed.

"But he's slobbering all over my car," Jude said in mock complaint.

"I can wash it," Gracie said.

Felicia chimed in. "I'll help."

Jude didn't answer. There would be zero chance he'd have these two lovelies doing something as messy as washing his car. Lovelies? He straightened in the seat, gripping the wheel to remind himself. *You're a cop. These two are your job. Don't get confused.*

Mind squared away, he parked on the curb outside Doc Howley's office. In the waiting room, he sat in a chair that faced the windows. Stretch obediently sprawled next to him, whining only slightly when the doctor greeted Gracie and Felicia.

"Shush, dog. You're to be on your best behavior, remember?" Just to be on the safe side, he scooted the box of crayons out of Stretch's sight.

Felicia reached for Gracie's hand, but the child hugged herself and looked at the floor. Jude's stomach twisted. Confusing for both of them. Was it a good thing for Felicia to create a bond with Gracie when she was only providing temporary housing? Especially if the DNA test proved they were not related and Keira had been untruthful for some unknown reason?

Felicia and Gracie followed the doctor into the exam room.

Jude's phone rang. "Dan. What's the news?"

"Keira's lawyer, Bernie Youngblood, has agreed to meet us at his Las Vegas office at one. Can you and Felicia make it?"

"Yes, if he doesn't mind a child and an elephant-sized dog crashing the party."

Dan laughed. "It'll be fine, I'm sure. This is already a pretty unorthodox meeting. I've lined up some questions to ask him."

"I've got a few of my own." He'd spent the wee hours before dawn checking out Bernie Youngblood and come up with nothing unusual. One driving under the influence infraction three years earlier on his way home from a Christmas Eve party. Otherwise, clean. "Any progress on locating Gracie's kinfolk?"

"The social worker and I are putting our heads together since her caseload is horrific. I've got the bare-bones facts so far. Keira was an only child, and both parents are deceased. She has a cousin living in Brazil, but it doesn't appear they're close." He paused. "This is going to be messy, Jude. You know there's more at stake with this DNA test than simply whether or not Felicia and Gracie are related. The test is also going to prove conclusively whether Keira was Felicia's birth mom."

"I know." Jude absently stroked Stretch's side. He'd realized that at some level, but the impact hadn't fully hit him. With one swab of the cheek, Felicia might find out that she and Gracie shared the same profound loss. It was possible that murder had taken a mother from both of them. How would Felicia handle it?

How had she handled almost dying? With grit and faith and as much humor as she could manage. But it was not without cost. What would be the cost of the DNA revelation? She was too young to have endured so much. Young in body, but wise in soul. Wiser than him, he feared. "Be there soon, Dan. Thanks for the info." He disconnected the call.

A shadow eased along the waiting room window. Jude turned in time to see the back of a man's head as he walked past on the sidewalk. Close-cropped hair, not unlike Jude's style, but dark. Medium build. Nondescript from the back in jeans and a long-sleeved T-shirt. Across the street was another man loading cardboard boxes into his pickup.

No cause for alarm on either count.

Another twenty minutes passed and Felicia returned with Gracie. Stretch bounded over to Gracie, yanking the leash clean out of Jude's fingers.

Jude hurried to grab it again.

Doc Howley nodded at Jude. "You've been promoted to chief dog wrangler?"

"So it would seem."

Doc smiled at Gracie. "Take care of Stretch, okay? Talk to you soon, Felicia."

"Gracie is healing like a champ, Doc says," Felicia told Jude after the doctor left. "She just needs to take it easy for another few days." She added softly, "He'll call us in the next week with the DNA results."

Jude told them about the meeting at the lawyer's office. "We'll need to scoot if we're going to make it by noon. I'd like to stop at home and switch out cars before we go. We'll be a bit less conspicuous and more comfortable. Gracie can play with Stretch for a minute before we load up again."

Felicia shot him a look. "Are you supposed to be doing this? Squiring us around on your day off? We can pick up my car and I can drive to the lawyer's."

"More room in my back seat for the mega beast," he said breezily. "I've got no other plans." Except painting his mom's spare bedroom, but he'd already called her to cancel. The excitement had been evident in his mom's tone.

"Oh, you're helping Felicia? That's so nice."

He'd tried to make it clear that helping and dating were two different things, but his mom had always adored Felicia and was crushed when he'd told her they weren't a couple anymore.

Felicia didn't say anything as they left the doctor's office.

Stepping into the sunshine dazzled his eyes, so he didn't at first see the man approach until Stretch belted out a deep woof.

The man in jeans with the dark hair. Much darker than the photo Jude had been shown.

From the front, his identity was clear.

Aaron Mattingly.

TEN

Felicia stared at the man whom she'd only seen in an image on Jude's phone. He was smiling broadly, wide cheeks flushed and eyes hidden behind sunglasses. His hair was unnaturally dark and there was the faintest chemical smell of dye. He held a cup of pink ice cream. His grin dimmed as Stretch barked furiously at him.

"That dog is such a pain in the rear." He slid the glasses to the top of his head. "Can't you control him?"

Jude held firmly to the leash. Felicia noticed Gracie had edged back a step, and Felicia leaned her hip out to subtly block Aaron's view of her.

"What do you want, Mr. Mattingly?" Jude said after he partially quieted the dog.

"I saw you all going into the doctor's office. I thought I'd get my little girl an ice cream. Strawberry. That's her favorite." He held out the cup.

Gracie stepped farther back, holding on to Felicia's waistband. Stretch's barks had become intermittent, but the dog was clearly still uneasy. Aaron frowned. "What's wrong? Can't a man give his daughter an ice cream?"

His daughter? The phrase sounded wrong. He wasn't her stepfather officially, but he had supposedly been in that parent role in Gracie's life. Felicia took the cup. "Thank you. She had a big breakfast."

"And to be clear, Mr. Mattingly, the topic of guardianship is still under consideration," Jude said.

"That's unfair. It was almost settled."

"Not officially," Jude said.

"I've been taking care of Keira and Gracie for three years. That's a long time. Paying bills and whatnot."

"Understood, yet Ms. Mattingly added a codicil at the last moment naming Felicia as Gracie's guardian. Any idea why she would do that?"

Aaron's mouth pinched, and then his expression became thunderous. "Yes, I was informed. It's a shame, really. Keira was mentally unstable, imagining affairs and all kinds of things. She took Gracie away for no reason and hid her from me with that woman in Mule Creek.

I tried so hard to find her, believe me. That's what we were arguing about when she took off." He shrugged. "Already told Sheriff Fox all that."

Felicia wished Gracie was not privy to the conversation.

Aaron stared at Felicia. "Are you some sort of blood relative I don't know about?"

The question of the hour, Felicia thought.

"That's being looked into," Jude said. "But there's a good chance."

Aaron's eyes roved over Gracie possessively before landing back on Felicia. "So you're taking her in?"

"I..." She swallowed. "Yes. For now."

"But you're a stranger."

It was the truth. She couldn't refute it.

"And you think it's okay to step in here and break up my family? Upend my plans? Why? What's your motive? So you can feel good about yourself? To take control of a child's money? You must have been in contact with Keira to set this all up behind my back."

Felicia's face burned hot. "I never even met Keira."

"Right. I'm supposed to believe that."

"Take it easy, Mr. Mattingly," Jude said as Stretch growled.

"I have the right to know." Aaron glared at Felicia. "Where are you keeping her, anyway? Your mother's house?"

Her pulse accelerated. He knew her mother had a house in town? Had he made the threatening phone call and maybe even upset Stretch in the yard?

"What are you doing in Furnace Falls?" Jude tightened his hold on the growling dog.

"On business."

"What business is that?"

"In the market for a used truck. Saw some listed in the paper, so figured I'd make a road trip of it. I needed something since I just lost my wife, and thanks to you, it looks like I'm losing my daughter, too."

"We have an appointment we've got to get to," Jude said.

"I need to know where my stepdaughter's being kept." Aaron's thick brows drew together. "I'm entitled to know that."

Jude seemed to grow taller, chin up, shoulders broad as a barn door. "Gracie was Keira's daughter, and she had the legal right to name whomever she wanted to be the guardian. You're going to need to accept that, Mr. Mattingly. She is not your stepdaughter in the eyes of the law."

"Her rights?" His eyes burned like twin coals. "What about *my* rights?" He stepped forward, but Stretch barked and lunged, sending him back a few paces. She saw the muscles work in his throat as he fought for composure. "That's not fair."

"Life's not fair." Jude's face was set like cement. "A grown-up like yourself must have noticed that."

"I'll be talking to my lawyer about what's to be done here. I haven't put in all this time and effort into raising a kid to be denied. And by the way, it's irresponsible to have a dangerous dog around a child. That monster outweighs Gracie by a hundred pounds. I told Keira the same thing."

"He's not a monster," Gracie piped up.

Felicia touched her shoulder.

"You can't take him away. Mommy said she wouldn't let you."

Aaron smiled slightly as if he'd earned a victory somehow. "I didn't want to take him away, sweetie. It was just for training, so you could be safe around him."

Gracie didn't reply, but Felicia felt her fingers tighten into claws. Very gently she reached around to put her palm on Gracie's head and shifted the tiniest bit more to further block Aaron.

"Go about your business, Mr. Mattingly," Jude said. His tone was knife-sharp. "That's not a request."

"All right." Aaron's voice was low and even. "But you won't take what's mine."

Felicia's heart hammered at the bright rage burning in Aaron's gray eyes, like pulsing storm clouds. *So easy*, she imagined him saying, and goose bumps rose along her arms before he finally stalked away. Stretch and Jude tracked him as he left.

Felicia turned around and knelt next to Gracie.

"I don't want that ice cream," Gracie said, and there was such emotion in her words that Felicia put the treat down on the sidewalk and wrapped her arms around the child. Gracie didn't return the embrace, but she did lean her head on Felicia's shoulder. "I don't wanna go with him. He was gonna send Stretch away. And he yelled at Mommy."

"It's okay." Felicia rubbed circles on Gracie's back. Stretch intruded his wet nose into their hug. "You don't have to go with him." She shot a questioning look to Jude, praying she was saying the right thing.

Jude gave a reassuring nod.

Gracie asked a question, her words muffled by Felicia's clothes. "Will I stay with you?" It was such a brittle voice, vulnerable and broken like tiny chips of glass sheared away from a fractured pane.

How Felicia's heart longed to ease Gracie's worry with a promise, but how could she? She might not even be Gracie's sister. And she hadn't agreed to become her parent. It was too much to ask. Too much.

"I…" She cast a terrified glance at Jude, whose expression was torn between supportive and helpless. "For now, okay? You and Stretch will stay with me for now."

Gracie didn't answer. She let go of Felicia and embraced Stretch's neck. The dog began to lick every available square inch of exposed skin. Jude offered a hand and Felicia took it, not sure she could get to her feet unassisted. What was she doing? Had she made a mistake taking Gracie until other arrangements could be made? Was she just going to deepen the child's loss? Dump another hurt onto the pile?

She remembered the cup of ice cream on the sidewalk and bent to pick it up when Stretch barged in. With a snap of his huge mouth, he ate the treat, cardboard cup and all. "Stretch," Felicia admonished.

Gracie laughed. "He likes ice cream." They

all joined in the laughter then, and the heaviness was momentarily lifted.

Thank you, Stretch. She hoped the cardboard cup didn't upset his stomach. Jude opened the passenger door for her, his gaze scanning the street for any sign that Aaron might be returning. He would remain vigilant, she knew, at least until he felt it was safe to go their separate ways. Was that okay? Could she stand being near him for another long day?

She couldn't treat him like a stranger, because she knew too much about him, had seen his tender side and been hurt by him. Now he was so embedded in the situation, there was no way she could shut him out completely.

Compromise. She'd allow him close again, close as in a helpmate, nothing deeper than that. Jude's purview was safety only. She'd press through her vulnerability and pray God would help her make the best decision she could for Gracie.

Gratefully she climbed into Jude's car, on the lookout for Aaron as they drove away.

Jude's phone rang as he rounded the last corner to his house.

"Saw your guy at the garage," Nora's husband, Seth, said.

"What? Aaron?" Jude put the call on speaker.

"Yes. I was dropping my car for a tire repair, and I saw him wandering around the lot."

Felicia gripped the seat-belt strap.

"Did he speak to anyone? Do anything?"

"No. He saw me watching him. I kept eyes on him until he left the lot."

"Thanks, Seth. Appreciate it."

"Anytime. Nora tells me Aaron's hassling women and children, and we can't have that, can we?"

"No, we can't. Thanks."

Jude called Fox.

"He was probably looking for Felicia's car," Jude said. Felicia went taut. He knew what she was contemplating. Was he thinking of planting a car bomb? Most likely not, but he didn't blame her for the thought. A memory of her lying in a hospital bed, bandaged and moaning in pain, assaulted him. He wouldn't let that happen to her again. No one was going to hurt Felicia if he had one ounce of fight left in him.

Simmer down, Jude. Not like she's your girl, right? Protection only.

"I'll head that direction now," Fox said. "Seems like he's staying in town. This morning he tried to check in at the Hotsprings, but Beckett turned him away. Figured he'd call over to Beatty probably, to try for a hotel room. I'm in court today, but I've got feelers out there and I'll know if he does." Fox paused. "Thanks for the intel, but I have this handled, Jude."

His tone was clear. *Butt out.*

"Right."

"I know you've got your Duke posse on the lookout. Remind them they should be feeding info to me, not you."

Teeth clenched, Jude bit back the retort he wanted to make and signed off as civilly as he could manage. Felicia stared out the window, lips pursed.

"The more eyes on Aaron, the better," Jude said, touching her lightly on the shoulder. "He won't be getting away with anything."

She didn't answer, so he could only hope his words had encouraged her. He was ready to change clothes, snag his civilian vehicle and head out to meet the lawyer. Fox wouldn't be happy about it, but Jude promised himself he'd provide every last detail about the meeting to his colleague.

It felt beyond strange to lead Felicia into his small home, where they'd eaten lunch the day before he'd broken up with her. A quiche he'd made from scratch. It had required two trips to the grocery store and a call to his mother to complete it. Nevertheless, she'd seemed to relish every bite, and he felt a ridiculous amount of pleasure watching her enjoy it. Too much pleasure, he'd realized. And then they'd gone to the Rocking Horse Ranch, and he could ignore his growing attachment no longer.

You shouldn't be with her.

She's Nora's best friend. She's too young.

Before Felicia, Jude had figured he'd probably live life alone, since he was stuck in his own ways, more gruff than gracious, bullheaded and blunt. If he did find a woman who was attracted to him, it wasn't going to be someone who'd eventually see the light and trot away to seek a more suitable match, like all the women his father had latched on to. What had they seen in Ron Duke? What could Felicia possibly have seen in Jude?

Doesn't matter. He led them into the kitchen. "Help yourself to whatever," he said. "Just gonna change into my civvies." In the bedroom, he pulled on a pair of soft jeans and a shirt loose-fitting enough to cover the belt holster. No way was he taking them anywhere unarmed. Not with Aaron nearby.

The guy was dirty. Jude knew it. And Aaron had no real love for Gracie. He knew that, too. Jude wasn't wired to parent, but he'd seen Beckett with his daughter, Fiona, and Seth with his nephew Peter, and Aaron's behavior was nothing like theirs. Jude was right about Aaron, and he intended to be sure Detweiler and Fox were convinced, too.

He returned to find Gracie and Stretch in the backyard, playing in the wide bare patch he had never bothered to landscape. They didn't seem to mind. Gracie'd found a stick to toss, and Stretch barreled to and fro like a freight train to retrieve it. Felicia was examining the photos on the oak sideboard he'd built. Her neck was slightly bent, and he could see the scar where she'd been burned by the car bomb. That scar would always remain; the invisible ones, too.

She turned. "Nora said you look like your father."

He stopped, unsure. "So I've been told, unfortunately."

She cocked her head. "She showed me a photo. He's handsome, so that's a compliment."

A block of hard-edged stone landed in his gut. "I want to be nothing like my father." He went to the kitchen and retrieved a bottle of water, which he offered her and she declined. He busied himself slugging some down.

She cocked her head and watched him until

he couldn't stand it anymore. "Was there something you wanted to say?"

"You didn't ever want to talk about your dad."

"Correct."

"It's partly why you broke up with me, isn't it?"

He felt as though he were the victim of a boulder falling from the sky. "What? No, I told you…"

"I know what you told me. Our age difference is a big deal to you because your father betrayed your mother with younger women. But I don't think that's all of it."

"Felicia…"

She held up a palm. "I've accepted that we aren't going to be together, Jude. You're right that our age gap is a factor, but there's more, isn't there?"

He felt his face go hot. "I don't need to be psychoanalyzed. Don't read anything into our breakup. We want different things, that's all."

Her eyes were strong and sad at the same time. "You never even asked me what I want, Jude. You assumed."

Had he? Assumed? Why were they having this conversation? Now, of all times? "You'll be happiest with someone your own age. Someone who knows the bands you listened to as a kid, who loves podcasts and live streaming, stuff I have no use for, and a guy your own age who doesn't give every moment to his job." Her expression didn't change, so he plowed on, desperate. "A guy with plenty of energy for a passel of children." He found her silence infuriating. "It wasn't about my father."

She didn't answer.

He couldn't bear her silent scrutiny for one more moment. "Say what you want to say, Felicia. You've always been honest. Let's have it."

"All right." After a moment's hesitation, she continued. "I think you're afraid of becoming your father."

Afraid? Of becoming his dad? "I'm not," he managed, shocked.

Her silence angered him.

"We broke up for good reasons. Maybe it's easier for you to think it's some mental problem on my part." Hard, unkind, the words made her flinch.

There was a long pause before she answered. "Right. Shouldn't have brought it up."

The room fell into silence except for the rushing of blood through Jude's veins. He stared mutely at her.

And then she let herself outside to play with

Gracie and Stretch, leaving him there with the empty bottle and his roiling gut. What had just happened? Her accusation had blindsided him. He'd broken up with her because of some emotional damage from his father? No way.

It was a practical and well-reasoned acknowledgment that they should not be together. Her Pollyanna thinking that love was enough to overcome all the differences between them was ludicrous. She would have sung a different tune if she and Jude had stuck together and she'd lost out on having a partner her own age who could share the same youthful enthusiasm and life goals. She should be all about travel and starting a family, not saddled with a jaded older cop who just wanted peace and quiet at the end of the day. The anger continued to bubble. She should be thanking him for saving both of them a lot of heartache. He'd done the right thing. He was sure of it.

He paced around the kitchen until he could get his emotions under control. Finally he grabbed his keys and called them.

"We should get going."

Felicia clipped the leash on Stretch. They got into Jude's Suburban, and he cranked the air conditioner. Hot under the collar, he realized. It was good that Felicia had aired her feelings, because it confirmed for him that he'd done the right thing in ending their relationship.

And what was more, he was doing the right thing again by protecting her and Gracie. Protecting was his job. Protecting was all he had.

Felicia's phone rang and she answered. "I am so happy to hear your voice, Uncle Abe. We're on our way to the lawyers now." She paused. "No. Jude's with me. I…um…" She eyed the back seat. "I can't talk right now, but I'll call you later, okay?"

He wondered if she was uncomfortable with talking in front of Gracie or him? It hurt, for some reason. Felicia had been the one person in his entire life he'd felt free and easy sharing with, up to a point. Sure, he'd dated before, but no one had ever gotten into his bloodstream the way she had.

Better that he hadn't shared any deep emotional stuff, since she seemed to have created a whole backstory for him in her imagination: the poor wounded man living in his father's shadow. Acid churned in his stomach at the thought. Pity was so much worse than disdain.

The two-hour drive to Las Vegas was a quiet one, and that was fine by him. When they pulled into the parking lot of the small office building, Gracie was asleep, with Stretch as her pillow. Dan's car was there already. Hopefully, Bernie Youngblood could give them some answers that would help Felicia decide what to do and maybe provide some info to help him catch Aaron.

Then there would be no need to continue the connection between him and Felicia. Teeth clenched, he got out.

Let's get this over with.

ELEVEN

Felicia took Gracie's hand and the child allowed it, probably because she was still groggy from her back-seat nap. Might she be hungry? She hadn't eaten since breakfast and it was edging closer to lunchtime. Felicia hadn't thought to bring along a snack. She'd been wrapped up in regret over her conversation with Jude. Why had she let it slip out that she suspected his actions had to do with past damage from his father? It wasn't her place to counsel him, nor did she want to. He'd walked out of her life and so she'd turned her back, too, and calloused her heart toward him. Not godly, but understandable. Wise, even, wasn't it? A clean break, if she'd only let it be.

A tiny thought nagged at her, though. Jude Duke was hiding the truth from himself. The pain of being cast off by his father still echoed in his life like a poorly played note. Totally his business, but knowing the valor he possessed, the compassion he'd shown to her and Gracie, she'd felt compelled to speak. Painful as it was, Jude wasn't hers to love, but she prayed he would find someone else with whom he could flourish.

Maybe you should try and focus here, Fee. The healed burn on the back of her neck felt tight in the noontime sun when they got out. No sunscreen, she realized, and she'd forgotten sunscreen on Gracie, too. She'd have to correct that mistake so Gracie could spend a few minutes outside later. Sunscreen in Death Valley was a requirement. Clearly she was not ready for this parenting business. At least Vera had agreed to drop off a box of Gracie's things on her way into town for a doctor's appointment. Gracie needed something familiar nearby in addition to Stretch.

The interior of the paneled office was blissfully cool. Nora rose from a chair. "Hiya. I drove Dan over." She held up a sack. "And I brought some coloring things so Gracie and I could entertain ourselves while you grown-ups chat about the boring stuff."

Stretch legged over for an ear rub, which Nora supplied until he began to nose at her pocket. She held up a chew bone. "And I didn't forget you, Super Stretch."

Felicia sighed with relief. She had not given a thought to packing along a coloring book. "Nora, you're the best."

She shrugged. "This is what I keep telling Seth." She cocked an eye at Jude. "What's wrong? You look like you swallowed a cactus."

Jude shook his head. "Nothing. Business face, is all."

"Hmm. Well, let me know if I can help out in any way."

He nodded. "Shall we?" he said to Felicia.

Felicia noted Nora's eyes fixed on her brother as a secretary led them to the conference room.

Dan sat at the rectangular table with an array of neatly stacked papers. He looked up as they entered. At the other end, a small man wearing a business shirt and his sleeves rolled up stood and offered a hand to them both.

"Bernie Youngblood," he said. His hair was neatly styled to make the most of a thinning patch on top. "Please sit down."

They took seats.

"I represent Keira Silvio Mattingly, as you already know." He frowned. "Terrible to hear of her death, especially with a young child left behind. Any word on how that happened?"

"Not yet," Jude said.

Bernie sighed. "A violent world, isn't it? All we can do is make the most of the time we have. Anyway, I've gone over the trust with Dan here since he is working with the authorities on this case. Normally, I wouldn't be so forthcoming with private information."

"I know we all appreciate your help." Dan touched an attachment on the earpiece of his glasses and a computer voice read a portion of the documents aloud while they all listened. After a moment, he put down the papers. "I went through the complete will earlier, thanks to Bernie's graciousness in giving me access. It's pretty standard. Keira and Aaron bought their house jointly, and upon her death it remains his, along with the contents. There is an additional trust worth…" He ruffled through some papers to hand them to Jude, but Bernie slid a packet over first to them.

"Here you go."

She leaned close to Jude to survey the contents. His aftershave was a subtle spice, a fragrance she'd missed more than she cared to admit.

"The trust is worth a little over twenty thousand dollars," Youngblood finished.

"That confirms what we already knew," Jude said. "Where'd the money come from?"

"Luca Silvio, Keira's first husband, asked me to start it with a settlement he'd received from Starlight Trucking for an on-the-job injury."

"What kind of injury?" Jude didn't look up from the papers.

"He broke his wrist on a truck door, the handle of which hadn't been repaired, though it had been reported multiple times, twice by Luca himself. It was a nasty break that required an orthopedist. The company wrote a check to settle. I drew up the trust that would have been overseen by Keira or Gracie's stepfather when the custody issue became finalized, but the codicil changes that." He looked curiously at Felicia. "Are you going to accept the guardianship? If so, you'll become the executor of that trust for Gracie's expenses. It always makes things easier to know there's financial help to support a child. Money eases all things."

Felicia wriggled in the chair. "I…haven't decided yet. There might be other people more suited."

Bernie nodded. "Perhaps. Keira didn't make provisions for any other family members, so I assumed…"

"Who would have been in control if Keira died before Aaron became the legal stepfather?" Jude asked.

"Me, acting as her default executor. Pretty standard in cases where there is no family." Bernie paused. "This isn't a matter of legal note, but perhaps of interest to your police investigation. Keira asked me several months ago if I could recommend a private investigator to locate a child she'd surrendered some twenty-seven years ago."

Felicia's heart beat fast as Youngblood looked at her curiously. "That's you, I presume."

Me. Keira's daughter.

"Did she tell you the results of that investigation?" Jude asked.

"I never heard, Felicia, but I assume, since you tell me that you received a photo of Gracie, that the investigator's report made her believe you are the child she left at the fire department."

The thoughts dropped into place one after the other. *Keira is likely my mother. Which means Gracie has to be my half sister at least.* Fear nibbled at her stomach. If Gracie was her relative, how could she possibly step in to raise her? Then again, how could she not? A list of her own shortcomings rattled in her brain. Too young, financially insecure, no experience with kids… *Oh, Lord*, she started, but the prayer died away. She tried to listen as the conversation continued.

"What do you think of Aaron Mattingly?" Jude said.

Youngblood considered, sipping from the coffee cup in front of him. "I met him only twice, once for the change in the will after they were married and a second time to start proceedings for the adoption."

"That's not an answer to my question," Jude said. "I'm asking for your assessment of his character."

Youngblood stared at Jude. "I'm not in the business of assessing character."

A careful lawyer answer. She felt Jude lean forward a fraction.

"We've got a murdered woman and a displaced child. Those two factors should outweigh your professional detachment, Mr. Youngblood."

Youngblood tapped a fingertip on the table. "Fair point. All right. I've never been married, myself, but he came across to me as a little too eager to show what a good husband he was. A tad…self-important, I guess you could say. And when we discussed the adoption application, he had to ask his wife Gracie's middle name." He shrugged. "It seemed odd to me that he loved the child enough to want to adopt her but he didn't know her middle name. Maybe that's not unusual. Like I said, I'm not a family man."

"It's Lita." Felicia felt all eyes swivel to hers. "Gracie's middle name. I asked her when we first talked." She cleared the lump from her throat. "It's my middle name, too."

Youngblood smiled. "Keira supplied that information for me as well." He paused. "It was her mother's name."

My grandmother? Mother, grandmother, sister... Felicia wished she could dart from the room and sort through it all in private instead of having three men examining her reaction as if she was a bug under a microscope. She tried to keep her demeanor calm and collected.

"Has Aaron contacted you recently?" Jude asked Youngblood.

"No."

"If he does, will you let us know?"

Youngblood cleared his throat. "To be perfectly honest, Sheriff, no. He's not been accused of a crime, and he is technically my client regarding the adoption, so there's an attorney-client privilege to be maintained."

"He's a threat," Jude snapped. "Isn't that more important?"

Dan spoke quietly. "Jude, Mr. Youngblood's got to follow the law just as much as you do."

Felicia heard Jude's molars grinding together as he shoved the papers into a pile in front of him. "All right. One last question. Are there any more significant assets at play here?"

Youngblood blinked. "Surely you're not suggesting I've failed to disclose? That would be a crime, too, Sheriff."

Dan shuffled his papers. "I am sure he wasn't implying you were hiding anything," he soothed. "We're just trying to pin down motive, I believe. Twenty thousand is not an exorbitant sum."

"Right." Jude didn't offer an apology. He was in his bull-in-a-china-shop mode. She'd seen it a few times when he'd thought she wasn't getting sufficient care at the hospital. She flashed back to a memory.

"Are you cold?" he'd asked, his navy blue eyes searching her face.

Cold, in pain, worn out. At the end of her endurance. At her nod, he'd taken a blanket from the chair to drape over her until she'd stopped him.

"Thank you, but it's just so scratchy." How whiny, she'd felt. Like a petulant child. *"I'll be fine."*

He'd disappeared without a word, returning

fifteen minutes later with a soft blanket printed all over with green cacti.

"The nurses only had more of the scratchy kind, but I found this one in the gift shop. I'll buy you something better, but for now is this okay?"

She'd fingered the fluffy fleece, heart warmed at the trouble he'd gone to. *"It's perfect. Thank you."* True to his word, he'd bought her another, an expensive, plush one, but that green cactus blanket was still on her chair at home. She refocused on Dan, who answered Jude's question.

"The Silvio Mattingly house in Las Vegas is small, in an inconvenient location, antiquated inside, according to the online photos posted. Aaron has already put it on the market. To be frank, it's not worth all that much. This trust account might be a motive for Aaron to go after Felicia, but…"

Youngblood frowned. "But it doesn't make much sense because I am the default executor, so he wouldn't assume that role anyway, even if Felicia was deceased. The adoption will definitely not go through now."

Dan cleared his throat. "There is another motive that could explain Aaron's actions where Felicia is concerned. Only one thing more motivating than money."

"Revenge?" Youngblood suggested.

"Bingo," Dan said.

Exactly what she'd suggested earlier. What was that saying? Revenge was a dish best served cold? Felicia realized her hands had gone icy. Aaron's words rang in her ears. *You won't take what's mine...* Would he go so far as to kill her because she'd interfered in his plan to adopt Gracie and take over her trust fund with such a moderate amount at stake? Was the loss of twenty thousand dollars enough to cause someone to commit murder?

You know it is. And then she was hurtling back in time, the car exploding in front of her, her hair on fire, her clothes smoldering as she fell.

She jumped, blinking, as she felt someone touching her. Jude was standing behind her, his big palm on her shoulder just below the scar. *You're okay*, his presence seemed to say. *You survived and you're here.* She forced a shaky breath in and out.

"You ready?" There was another question in it, a deeper one. *Are you able to keep going with this?* But she couldn't answer that one, not at the moment. Her feelings about the fact that she'd probably lost her biological mother before she'd even known her would have to be put on the shelf for another time when she had the luxury to deal with them. Right now, there was a child waiting for someone to take care of her, no matter how temporary that might be. All she could do was mumble a thank-you and get to her feet, trail after Jude and Dan from the conference room to rejoin Nora, Gracie and Stretch.

Gracie and Nora were playing a spirited game of tic-tac-toe on a notepad. Gracie pumped a fist in the air. "I won!" she crowed. And then immediately added, "But you played real good."

Nora laughed and gave Gracie a high five. A lovely moment.

Felicia swallowed hard against a wall of threatening tears. Gracie was supposed to be a little kid having fun with supportive people around her, like Felicia had experienced her entire childhood. Instead her destiny was in the hands of Felicia and the courts. Aaron was circling like a hungry vulture for some reason, shadowing Gracie's life.

Not fair.

Then another notion followed.

And nothing else is going to happen to her. She had to protect this child, and after Jude dropped them off back home, it would all be on her shoulders. Jude's gaze lingered as he stood next to Dan, muscular arms folded across his chest. How she'd ached to have Jude standing by her side, a partner in her triumphant return to life after the explosion. Another loss that she was still teaching herself to withstand.

You're going it alone, Felicia. Better be strong. Thanking Nora, she reached a hand out to Gracie. This time, the child took it.

Jude drove them back to Felicia's house. Felicia was silent and he wished she would say something, anything. *Think about what she's just heard about the woman who is likely her mother. Get over yourself, why don't you? She doesn't have to deal with things the way you do.*

Or didn't, maybe? Felicia's accusation still stung. *You're afraid of becoming your father.* He'd kept his own father out of his mind through iron will. But not wanting to repeat his dad's mistakes didn't mean he was fearful of actually turning into the man. Distracted, he saw a cardboard box with "Gracie" written on the side on Felicia's front porch as they drove up.

Gracie started to run with Stretch to check it out, but Jude got there first. Eyes riveted on Jude, Felicia took the leash from Gracie. "Gracie, wait. We'll let Sheriff Duke carry that, okay?"

"She can call me Jude," he said, hefting the carton.

Gracie didn't respond and he figured she didn't want to call him anything, since he'd stepped between her and her toys. *Sorry, kiddo*, he thought, hoping he hadn't been gruff. After the two went inside, he put the box on the porch step and quickly went through it.

It felt strange, pawing among the small treasures: a ratty bunny rabbit, a set of books about horses, a framed photograph of a toddler Gracie, Keira and a tall, lanky man with a broad smile who must be Luca. The three of them looked as though they belonged together, a happy family. For a split second he imagined what it would be like to stand in a photo with his own wife and child, but the vision wobbled, and instead he pictured his father, smiling, charming, lovable, until he'd gambled away his mother's savings and, worse, taken up a series of relationships with women half his age. Disgust tasted like acid in his throat, and he felt again the sting of Felicia's words.

But she was wrong. He would *never* be anything like Ron Duke. He simply had a healthy disregard for his dad's failure, and there was nothing wrong with that. Jude was gruff, blunt and too old for Felicia Tennison, but he wasn't and would never be Ron Duke. Case closed.

He finished rummaging through the toys and found nothing unexpected, so he carried the box inside and placed it near Gracie, who was folding paper napkins for lunch. She hastily put the napkins on the table and knelt on the floor to look inside the box. Stretch sat with her, his attention torn between the contents of the box and the smell of peanut butter.

Jude's stomach growled so loudly it made Stretch bark. "Sorry."

"No need to be sorry," Felicia said. "You've been with us all day. The least I can do is make you a peanut-butter-and-jelly sandwich."

A snack before he hit the road. "That'd be nice. Give me a minute to fill Fox in and I'll join you." He made the phone call, got Fox's voice mail and left a detailed message. By the time he was done, there was a beautifully plump peanut-butter-and-strawberry-jelly sandwich waiting for him. Stretch whined. Probably wishing he had his own sandwich. Jude took a big bite and closed his eyes.

"Why is peanut butter and jelly so good?" he said.

Felicia laughed. "One of nature's mysteries."

Gracie's had the crusts removed as he'd remembered Vera doing with her toast. Felicia must have noticed that detail. Not surprising. She was perceptive, but not about everything. His gaze drifted to the front door. There was a sturdy bolt. He wondered if he could convince her to install an alarm system before he left. Her mother, Olivia, would probably agree in a heartbeat to anything that would keep Felicia safe after she'd come so close to losing her.

Now Stretch was circling the cardboard carton, shoving his head inside, tail whipping madly from side to side.

"Is there a ball in there for him?" Felicia asked around a bite of sandwich.

Gracie shook her head. "No. Miss Vera forgot to pack Stretch's toys."

"I think Austin sent some. I'll find him a ball after lunch."

The dog continued to fuss. Jude wiped his mouth and got up. "All right, boy. What's the problem here? Is there a dog biscuit on the bottom that I missed maybe?"

Stretch looked at Jude full-on and barked once. More urgency in that one bark than a whole human sentence. Nerves tingling, he said, "Felicia, please take Gracie outside for a minute, okay?"

Felicia didn't question. She immediately gathered Gracie, and they opened the front door. Gracie was still holding her sandwich as she passed by Jude. He smiled at her. "Everything's fine, I promise. Just want to check something. I'll come get you in a quick second."

"Stretch," Gracie called.

"Stretch is gonna help me check. He's a real smart dog, isn't he?"

Gracie nodded uncertainly.

He knew he'd scared her, but he had to get them out of the house until he calmed his own nerves. Something in the box had attracted the dog's attention. It was probably nothing, but he wasn't going to take the chance.

When they were clear, he tipped the box on its side. Stretch dived in immediately with such force that he almost knocked the box away from Jude.

"Whatcha got, Stretch?"

The dog nosed the stuffed rabbit out of the way while Jude decided on a plan. If there was any sign of an explosive or other danger, he'd manhandle Stretch outside and call the bomb squad, but it could just as easily be that a rodent or cat had left a scent, or a piece of food the chowhound was after.

Stretch bonked his nose on something hard, sniffing and scratching at it. Jude pulled him aside enough to see. The photo of Keira, Luca and Gracie.

Swiping a paper napkin, Jude gingerly eased the frame from the box, setting it glass side down on the floor. With his free arm, he shoved Stretch away.

"Sit," he commanded. The dog dropped to a discontented sprawl on the floor.

The frame was a cheap wooden one, meant to stand on a table. There did not seem to be anything amiss about it until he looked closer under the stand. His breath caught.

"Stretch, you are worth your weight in kibble," he said as he reached for his cell phone.

TWELVE

Jude opened the door for Felicia and Gracie after he'd photographed the frame and moved it to the kitchen counter to keep it away from the dog. Stretch, a canine bottomless pit, had to be distracted with a half dozen dog treats. Jude had also reexamined each of the other toys in minute detail to be sure he hadn't missed anything the first time.

"All clear." He kept what he hoped was a sunny smile on his face. Jude had been told his fake smiles were scarier than a menacing leer, but he figured it was worth a try. This all had to add to the confusion for the poor kid.

Outside, Felicia's face was chalky and she gripped Gracie's hand, unmoving. The child looked from Felicia to Jude and back to Felicia again. He repeated the invitation to come inside, but still Felicia didn't move.

He hustled out and bent toward Gracie as

Stretch loped over to his small master. Gracie let go of Felicia's hand and crouched to scratch her enormous companion. Stretch licked at the traces of peanut butter on Gracie's skin.

"See there? Stretch was wondering where you went," Jude said.

While Gracie was occupied, Jude stepped close to Felicia. She was breathing fast, her throat convulsing with panicked swallowing. Using one finger, he tipped her chin to meet his gaze.

"Fee, listen. Everything is safe now."

"Did he...? Was it a bomb?"

"No. No bomb." He locked his gaze to hers. "You can trust me."

He shouldn't have picked that phrase, but he meant it. She could trust him—with this, anyway. Was that a glimmer of tears in the depths of her eyes? He allowed his thumb to graze the satin of her cheek to draw her back from the hideous memories of what she'd endured. Words wouldn't help, but maybe his touch would. "I promise you are safe."

She seemed to lean into him for a microsecond. Everything in him longed to sweep her into an embrace, reassure her and himself. His heart twisted in his chest, beating in a rhythm he could not control, until she took a deep breath and eased away. "Sorry. I was just... I'm okay."

"Post-traumatic stress. Completely understandable." He'd experienced it himself after some nasty work situations. He figured every cop had, but many simply wouldn't talk about it, like himself. It seemed to him that remembering the trauma could hurt almost as much as experiencing it the first time. Still, he could never predict when past events would intrude on the present.

After a couple of deep breaths, she followed him into the house with Gracie and Stretch bringing up the rear. He made sure to enter first, crossed the kitchen and leaned casually against the counter to block Gracie's view of the photo. It wasn't easy to hide things from a six-year-old. Felicia stared at him, and he gave her a slight head jerk. She understood the nonverbal hint.

"Umm, Gracie, since you finished your sandwich, can you go wash your hands in the bathroom? And I think I left a ball for Stretch in your room last night in one of the drawers. Maybe you can find it."

Gracie nodded and disappeared with Stretch. Felicia joined him at the kitchen counter.

"Okay. Let's hear it." Her voice wavered only a tiny bit. "What's wrong?"

He moved aside and showed her the frame, pointing to the sliver of duct tape underneath the stand. "A GPS tracker."

Felicia gaped. "How...?"

"I'm thinking Aaron drove by the house after he went to the garage. His intention was probably to put a tracker on your vehicle, but he saw Seth watching him and he couldn't. He noticed the box of belongings on the porch from Vera and came up with plan B."

"But why would he do that? What is the point of tracking us?"

Jude frowned. "Not sure about his motives, but the method was clever. He knows you wouldn't take Gracie anywhere without that photo of her mother and father. I wouldn't have found it if Stretch hadn't smelled it. He doesn't like Aaron one iota."

"Are we still thinking Aaron's looking to kill me out of revenge? Or does he still think he's somehow going to be awarded custody if I'm out of the picture?"

"I don't know. I'm hoping Fox can clarify the motive. My assignment is safety."

A job he'd given to himself. And seeing her frozen in abject terror at the thought of an explosive in Gracie's toys, he knew he was right. God had put him in Felicia's life again to protect her, and he was going to see it through. The sense of duty would overshadow any romantic regret.

She put a shaky hand to her mouth. "I feel like we're being hunted. What…what should I do?"

The very question he'd been mulling over. The answer was clear in his mind, but he was determined to present it as a choice, not a demand. He resisted the urge to pull her to him. *Duty, remember?* "Felicia, with Aaron looking for a way to track your location, it's no longer safe here. You and Gracie need to leave."

"Leave? But this is my mom's house. I have to go back to work at some point. And Gracie needs to be near her doctor."

When she took a breath to continue, he plowed on. "A good option is to go to your uncle's campground for a while."

She reached up to twirl her hair, a leftover habit from the days before it was burned away and she'd gone to a pixie cut. "At Sidewinder Springs? It's kind of remote. Do you think it would be safe to take her there?"

He gulped in a breath. "It will be, if I accompany you two."

She frowned. "No, Jude. We've been through this."

He tried to keep his tone light and approachable. Not the time for grit. "I understand you're absolutely capable of taking care of yourself and Gracie. And I know it's Fox's case, but he's got a killer workload and he can't devote enough attention to you two."

"Detweiler doesn't want you involved."

"I know, but she's always on me about how much vacation I have on the books. I might as well spend some of it at a campground." He gave her a playful grin. "You used to tell me something about this guy named Jack."

Now he got the smile he'd been working for.

"All work and no play makes Jack a dull boy."

"That's the one. A vacation is just what this dull boy needs." He added, "It's not a long-term thing, Fee. Just until we have enough to bust Aaron or your mom comes back so you aren't alone with Gracie."

Felicia blew out a breath. "I'm going to be honest. It's…uncomfortable to be around you, Jude."

The comment punctured like a nail right into his heart, though he knew he deserved the injury. "I get it. I'll keep this as professional as I can. I'm a bodyguard, is all. An extra set of eyes and hands."

She cocked her head in that birdlike way she had when she was considering something, and again his heart lurched.

"And I'm your assignment? Nothing more."

There was the tiniest shade of uncertainty hidden in the question, which gave him pause.

Could he actually treat Felicia as if she was an assignment only? When she awakened such a bushel of conflicting feelings for him? "Absolutely," he heard himself say. The Lord would help him do what was needed to protect them. That was all that mattered.

She looked around helplessly. "Or maybe I could leave the state. Go to Colorado with Gracie, get my old job back at the donkey rescue headquarters."

"Not until the custody situation is resolved."

"But that might take…"

"A few weeks at least." He paused. "Unless you've decided to accept guardianship."

"Honestly, I still don't know what to do. Until the DNA comes back…"

"We need to keep you and Gracie safe. The campground is the best answer." *If I'm there as security.* Was that his pride talking? Or something else?

Her gaze wandered from him to the GPS tracker.

"All right," she said finally.

He did his best to hide his relief.

"But what do we do about this thing?" She peered at the minuscule device taped to the frame.

"As far as Aaron's going to know, you and

Gracie are staying right here." He winked. "There's a plot afoot."

To his surprise, she laughed, a hearty belly laugh. "Reminds me of your debut as Sherlock Holmes for the hospital party."

Toward the latter stage of her recovery, the hospital had hosted a costume event for the kids where everyone was to show up as a book character. Felicia had tried to be Stuart Little with some ears procured by Nora, but they'd proved so painful with her burns that she'd had to take them off. His mortification at showing up in full Sherlock Holmes regalia vanished the moment he'd seen her face light up.

"Anything for the kids," he'd said, but he hadn't donned a costume only for them. Not really. He'd done it for the one person in the world who could make him unafraid to be silly: Felicia. His eyes roved her face seeking the curve of her smile, the same delicate beauty, but stronger now for all the scars she bore. Stronger...but scared.

That was what he could do for her. Control the situation so she didn't have to be afraid. *Aaron Mattingly, you won't win. Ever.*

"You're a good man, Sherlock," Felicia said softly.

A good man? After he'd dumped her? Hurt her? Maybe not, but a good cop was what she needed, and that was a role he could play. He found he wanted to hold her close, listen to her soft breathing and feel the tickle of her hair on his chin. A daydream so palpable it was painful. What was he thinking?

"I'll make some phone calls," he said, relieved and saddened to put some space between them.

It took Jude some time to explain the ruse of leaving the GPS in the house to Fox before Felicia called her uncle.

"I'm in, one hundred percent," Uncle Abe said. "I've got a cabin with two bedrooms and a couch that won't be rented until November." He paused. "I'll get it ready right now. We don't technically open for another week, so it's basically me and some staff. Pretty empty."

Empty? Would that leave them more of a target or less? If Aaron found them… But Jude would make sure that didn't happen. "As long as the animals are still there, Gracie will be thrilled."

"Five horses Levi Duke helps me manage and the two rescued donkeys you and Nora arranged for us to get. The swimming pool's ready, too, if her wound is healed enough that she can be in the water."

Felicia made a mental note to ask the doctor about swimming.

Uncle Abe cleared his throat. "Honey, I know this is a stressful time for you. You sure you don't want to call your mom?"

"Mom needs to be with her sister. I'm okay. Really. Figuring things out one day at a time."

"That's all we can do. See you soon, baby."

She hung up, her uncle's warmth echoing in her heart. Maybe it was going to be all right. But how would she handle Jude watching their every move in the cabin when she found her thoughts trending more and more in his direction?

The doorbell chimed, and she heard Jude let Nora and Seth inside. She hugged her best friend close. Nora, a head taller than Felicia, returned the squeeze.

"Audrey's all fixed and parked outside. I'll help you pack up some things. And my mom sent these over." Nora wiggled a tin. "Chocolate chip and walnut. Jude's favorite, but she figured they'd go over well with you and Gracie, too."

Nora and Felicia watched as the GPS tracker was photographed.

"A crime scene tech in civilian clothes and car will arrive later to examine it for prints, on the off chance there are any." Jude slid the photo out and put it in another frame Felicia had found in the garage.

"So you're going to make the house look occupied?" Nora asked while Seth installed the timers they'd picked up on the bedroom and living room lamps.

"As best we can," Jude said. "Lights on and off. GPS tracker still active. Her car in the driveway. It's not foolproof, but it might buy some time for Fox to continue the investigation."

"And you're acting as what? A bodyguard?" Nora said.

Jude didn't quite look at his sister. "Affirmative."

Nora shot a quick glance at Felicia, but she kept her face even. Later in the bedroom, Nora cornered her. "So...you and Jude will be in close proximity for a while, huh?"

She nodded, folding Gracie's T-shirts and putting them into a duffel bag.

"And how are you feeling about that?" Nora's intense blue gaze was so like Jude's.

"It's not optimal, but I'm making the best of it."

Nora sighed. "As long as you're not being steamrolled. Jude can be stubborn as an ox."

"I'm aware, but he's got a softer side." After a hesitation, she told Nora what she'd said to

Jude. "I offended him when I said he was afraid of turning into his father."

"I've thought the same thing from time to time. Dad's decisions rocked our world in ways we're still finding out. I've wondered what it's like for Jude as a man, having his role model do something like that. He and I have only recently reconciled, of course, but when I broach the subject, he immediately shuts me down." Nora went silent a moment and then she smiled. "But you actually told Jude that, and he still wants to stick close to you? That took some guts, or grit, as Jude would say. Maybe you and my brother really were meant to be together, in spite of his silly notions to the contrary."

"No." Felicia swallowed the lump in her throat. "We weren't."

"No feelings left?"

She could not escape Nora's prodding. Her friend would see through any smoke screens.

"Plenty of feelings, but no future."

"Are you sure?"

"One hundred percent. He was right. There are too many differences between us and I'm not opening myself up to him again, not fully." She snagged a stack of pants to pack. "Lately, I don't know which end is up, and I have to focus on keeping Gracie safe. My life is all about her and no one else."

"Okay."

She was relieved when Nora dropped the subject.

"Seth and I are going to follow you to the campground from a distance to be sure Aaron isn't around if Fox doesn't have an exact location on him."

"And what if Aaron is lurking and he spots you?"

Nora laughed. "I'm a Duke, Felicia. We know how to handle ourselves, remember?"

Nora was a crack shot and a fiercely determined person, the perfect complement to easygoing Seth. It warmed Felicia to see them together…a solid couple, devoted to each other, yet with distinct personalities.

Finished packing, she followed Nora to the kitchen, where they listened to Fox's report on the speakerphone. "Aaron's car's not at the hotel, according to my sources, so he's out of pocket for the moment. Eyes peeled, huh?"

Felicia resisted a shiver. The GPS tracker lay innocently on the kitchen counter. They'd better watch their backs, because she had a feeling Aaron was somewhere close by, doing exactly the same thing.

THIRTEEN

The drive took them far out into the foothills, a few miles from the western border of Death Valley National Park. They passed only a couple of vehicles, but Jude knew from experience that the traffic would pick up a tick since fall was the beginning of the busy tourist season. Death Valley was the most beautiful place in the world, but not many could stomach the summer temps that could easily top 120 degrees. Salt dunes, sand flats, mountains— the valley had it all, but the wide-open spaces spoke to Jude's soul.

Felicia's, too, he knew from previous experience. He loved the way she rolled down the window and let the hot air billow in, along with the scent of blackbush and mesquite.

Gracie spotted the wooden sign for Sidewinder Springs Campground. "Are we there?"

"Just about." Jude slowed, easing the car from

the paved road onto a long gravel entrance. Stretch shoved his face out, lips flapping in the wind as they rolled past the scrubby trees. Next to the wood-sided lodge was a swimming pool, glittering in the brilliant light. A man wearing a Sidewinder Springs T-shirt was fiddling with the pump.

Uncle Abe met them at the office, scooting from behind a countertop covered with informational flyers and pamphlets. Jude immediately warmed to the silver-haired man with the sun-wrinkled skin.

"Thank you." Abe gripped Jude's hand. "For helping Felicia. She's always been my treasure and her mother's, too."

Before he could figure out exactly how to reply, Abe was hugging Felicia, chatting with Gracie and admiring Stretch. Greetings finished, he led them past the dozen log cabin–style structures and pointed out the corrals and coin-operated laundry, the showers in three locations on the property and a tiny grocery store stocked with sundries.

"Not open just yet, but we can probably rustle up whatever you need," he said. Stretch galloped to the corral, where he was ignored by the horses and donkeys who were more interested in greeting Gracie, a possible source of treats.

She laughed in delight when they snuffled at her pockets. The high-pitched squeal made him chuckle in response. It struck him that he'd only heard her laugh a few times before, and it warmed his insides to hear it. *Thanks, God, for giving her a moment of joy.* He realized he was honored to bear witness to it.

The farthest cabin was another squat, wood-sided structure with a rustic bench on the tiny front porch. Abe pushed the door open, releasing a puff of stale air.

"No dead bolt?" Jude said.

Uncle Abe frowned. "Afraid not, but there's a bar that can be slid down once you're inside. We're an old-school campground here, but we do actually have cell service. That's important to our visitors since we exist for kids with medical issues." He checked his watch. "Speaking of which, I have a phone appointment to discuss needs for a client in a minute or two. See you at dinner." He kissed Felicia and offered a courtly handshake to Gracie, which made her giggle.

Jude searched the area behind the cabin, a flat expanse of dry, rocky terrain that stretched into the distance where the mountains rose up to scrape the late-afternoon sky. Sweat prickled his brow as he surveyed. The property wasn't fenced, unfortunately. Two of the cabin's windows looked out onto this landscape. Those windows would be secured even if he had to saw a broomstick in half to provide the stops.

Gracie and Stretch emerged from the cabin to check out the open space, and he hustled right along with them. "See that big rock?" He pointed to a sandy pinnacle the size of a small car.

Gracie nodded.

"Don't go past it, okay? So you and Stretch won't get lost."

She nodded, frowning at her index finger.

"Something wrong, Gracie?"

"Hurts."

He took a knee and examined. "Ah, I see. Got yourself a sliver here. No prob. I'm an old pro at splinter removal." Swallowing his pride, he slid on a pair of reading glasses and squinted. "Here it is." He plucked out the sliver. "Better?"

She smiled, setting the splash of freckles across her nose dancing. "Thank you, Mr. Judy. I got a friend named Judy."

"My name's Jude," he said gently. "Close to Judy."

She pursed her lips. "Are you sure?"

He laughed at her seriousness. "Yes, ma'am. Just Jude." Gracie was adorable, he had to admit. But she would be gone out of his life soon, too, like Felicia. The notion sent a burst of cold through him in spite of the heat. No more Gracie. No more Felicia. He'd only spent a few days with them. Why was the thought of their departure so disconcerting? "How about we unpack your stuff in your room? Stretch will want to know where you're going to stow his toys and treats."

They trooped back into the cabin. Felicia had the ceiling fans spinning to dispel some of the stuffiness. A small air conditioner in the corner did not look promising, but he cranked it on anyway. It rattled and wheezed to life.

"Uncle Abe says we can eat in the dining hall with the staff at five." Felicia handed Gracie her small pack. The child scampered to her room.

"Good to see her look happy for a minute, even if she does think my name is Judy."

"'Judy Duke' has a nice ring to it," she teased. Her phone rang. "I don't recognize the number. Should I answer?"

"Let me." Jude took it from her. "Sheriff Duke."

Silence. The tiny muscles in his stomach snapped tight. He didn't need to be told the person on the other end was Aaron Mattingly. He could feel it. Felicia grabbed his shoulder, her fingers cold through the T-shirt material. "Is it him?" she mouthed.

Jude ignored her, fury sweeping over him. He gripped the phone as his blood heated to a boil. "You're not going to touch Felicia or Gracie."

Silence unspooled between them, prickly as a roll of barbed wire.

"You always get your way, right?" the voice said. He didn't identify himself, but Jude knew anyway. Aaron. He'd be calling from a burner phone. "In school, in your job. Now you think you can be the boss of everyone else, too."

"Only the bad guys."

"I'm not the bad guy. I did my time being married, didn't I? Did the father bit for a kid who wasn't even mine?"

Jude swallowed his disgust. "You never deserved either of them."

"You don't know anything about it. Trust me on this, though. I don't forget, and I don't forgive. My plans were ruined, and I will exact payment for that."

"Not. Gonna. Happen."

"You're so tough over the phone, aren't you, Sheriff? But it's a real big desert, and you're just a small-town cop. I'll do what I set out to, and I'll have an alibi every step of the way so you won't ever be able to prove a thing. You're not going to stop me."

"Wrong." The rage almost choked off the word.

"Sit back and wait, Sheriff. And you know what's even better?" His voice dropped to a poisonous whisper. "It's going to be so easy and you won't even see it coming. You'll live with the knowledge that you weren't fast enough or smart enough to catch me." The connection ended.

Jude immediately texted the number to Fox to check it out, though it would be futile. A verbal threat without ironclad identification was not going to be enough to make an arrest. Besides, it would anger both Fox and Detweiler that Jude was continuing to insert himself into the investigation. No help for that. He could deal with their anger as long as Felicia and Gracie were safe. Aaron was now issuing direct threats, which would earn him a long conversation with law enforcement, if nothing else. When he finished, Felicia was staring at him. "Aaron's found us?"

"No. The call doesn't mean he knows where you are. He's blowing smoke, is all. Enjoying the power of scaring you." The coward.

"He's doing a really good job of that."

On impulse, he reached out and laced his fingers through hers. "Don't let him get in your head. He's not going to touch you or Gracie. That's why I'm here, remember?"

She clutched his hand. "I… I'm grateful, if I didn't say so before. You didn't have to become involved in all this."

Oh, but he did. Even the thought of Felicia being in trouble left him powerless to do anything but commit his entire being to helping her. He didn't understand it, but at that moment he had to admit it.

"Come on," he said with a final squeeze of her hand. "Let's take Gracie to look at the horses on our way to the chow hall. I'm starved."

Stretch wasn't allowed in the eating area when they arrived, so he waited unhappily outside. Jude figured Stretch would be a great help if Aaron did come around. Stretch had a deep dislike for the man. *Good boy.* Waiting wasn't too bad when Uncle Abe provided a rope toy for the dog to maul on the porch. Over brisket, slabs of buttered bread and salad, Jude introduced himself to the few staff members. "Friend of Felicia's," he said to explain his presence. "Helping out with the stables next week for Uncle Abe."

Felicia was polite but quiet, eating sparingly, cutting Gracie's meat and encouraging her to sample some vegetables. He made sure their water glasses were emptied by the end of the meal. Dehydration wasn't a trivial matter in the Mojave.

After dinner, another walk around the campground left Gracie dragging. Poor kid probably hadn't gotten a good night's sleep since she left Vera's house. He reminded himself she was supposed to be taking it easy. "Want a ride?" Jude said impulsively.

Gracie nodded, and he hefted her onto his shoulders. She clasped him around the chin.

"New hat." She tapped his baseball cap.

"I had to use my spare since Stretch chewed my other one."

"He's real sorry." Gracie patted Jude on the cheek.

Strange satisfaction flooded through him as they headed back to the cabin and settled into their rooms. There was something about the scenario that tugged at his insides. Odd, for a man with no family aspirations. Jude assumed the role of uncle to Beckett and Laney's baby and to Levi and Mara's newborn, but he felt something different with Gracie. Paternal? Not like he'd inherited any great skills in that department.

He found a broomstick and borrowed a saw from Uncle Abe to fashion two window stops. Not as good as bolts, but better than nothing.

The day eased into dusk with only a brief message from Fox.

No trace on phone.

No surprise there.

Aaron's Las Vegas house and the hotel in Beatty where he was staying were under watch. No sign of him in either place. *You'll live with the knowledge that you weren't fast enough or smart enough to catch me.*

Teeth clenched, Jude took the sofa and watched the moments tick by on the old mantel clock. The ceiling fan spun lazily but didn't dispel the stuffiness of the room any more than the air conditioner. He mentally shuffled through the details of the case, deciding to call Dan again in the morning. Something about the situation prodded him, but he couldn't pinpoint the source. Or maybe it was residual nervous energy from having Felicia so close. In the past he'd painted her image clearly in his mind—too young, too carefree, Nora's best friend… But now the picture was changing. He couldn't ignore that the woman thirteen years his junior was plenty mature, selfless and courageous, a person he was developing intense feelings for.

No. No way. You burned that bridge, and she doesn't want you. And he didn't want a relationship, either, did he? Or did he?

He pondered again what she'd said earlier about him being afraid to become his father. Fear? He'd never been afraid of anything in his life. But what made him refuse to think about his father, purposely eschewing anything Ron Duke embodied? Everything from bowling, to drinking soda pop…to dating younger women? Was it disdain, like he'd told himself? Or fear? Sweat dampened his brow. Suddenly he felt like he was suffocating in the sultry room.

A high-pitched whinny snagged his attention. He bolted up, listening. Another, softer sound, the movement of hooves. He'd been around horses long enough to decipher their moods. Agitation. His phone told him it was nearly 1:00 a.m. So what would upset the horses at that hour? Perhaps a mountain lion come down to the flats in search of a meal?

He pulled on his boots and strapped on his sidearm.

Felicia poked her head from the bedroom.

"I heard you moving around. What is it?" she whispered.

"Stay here with the doors locked."

"Jude." She hurried to him, small in her leggings and T-shirt, feet bare.

He meant to press a kiss to her cheek before he could rethink it, but she moved so his lips brushed hers, an electric spark dancing up his arms. "Gonna be okay," he whispered into her hair. "Be right back."

Senses tingling from the kiss, he let himself out.

He sucked in a deep breath to clear the fuzz from his mind. There was no way to keep to the shadows as he approached the stables. The moonlight bathed the open space in silver light. He could see that the corral gate was open. He drew his weapon and eased close. The heat of the day had faded into a heavy warmth that seemed to hold on to the sounds of his footsteps and recirculate them in the air. Listening, he stopped, then restarted, one cautious footstep at a time.

Two feet from the gate, the horses exploded from the corral. He darted to the side as the animals thundered past.

His first thought was to press his way through.

If Aaron was responsible, Jude would get him. Finally.

But then another thought took its place.

Aaron would have spooked the horses as a diversion.

Whirling on his heel, he raced back to the cabin.

Felicia waited in Gracie's room with the fireplace poker in her hand. Stretch was alert, watching as he sprawled over the sleeping Gracie's legs. The door was barred, she told herself. No one could get in. Her heart slammed her ribs. What about Jude? Would he be out there, easy prey for Aaron? Should she text her uncle? But if he came running, it would be dangerous for him and for Jude. The police would be too far from this distant spot to intervene. She wanted to look out the window, but she knew that wasn't a safe choice.

Instead she murmured a prayer and gripped the poker. If Aaron somehow managed to get in, how would she fend him off with a flimsy fireplace poker? *What are you going to do? Bash him on the head?*

That was exactly what she'd try with every last ounce of her strength to keep him away from Gracie, she thought with a rush.

Something brushed the exterior bedroom wall and her breath caught. Stretch growled low, seeming to grow larger in the faint streak of moonlight that peeked through the curtains. Stretch, too, would do anything to protect Gracie. It was some comfort to have the one-hundred-plus-pound dog at her side. The poker bit into her clammy palm. Seconds ticked into minutes, five, ten, fifteen.

With a snarl, Stretch leaped at the window, his nails catching the fabric of the curtain. Gracie sat up with a scream.

Felicia dropped the poker, swept her up and ran from the room. She watched, panting through the bedroom door, as Stretch stood on hind legs, peering out the window.

Gracie buried her head in Felicia's chest, her wails muffled.

"I'm here. It's okay." Was it? Would Jude protect them? Had he been hurt? Or worse? All she could do was hold Gracie and pray. Was that the sound of running feet or her own panicked breathing? She simply could not think of a plan of escape. After a final growl, Stretch trotted out of the bedroom and over to the sofa, shimmying close to nose at Gracie.

Did that mean the threat was gone?

A text vibrated her phone. She eased Gracie onto the sofa.

"Are you going away?" Gracie clutched her arm.

Felicia knelt next to her, holding her frightened gaze. "No. I'm not leaving you."

Gracie nodded, her mouth still tight with fear. Stretch crawled up next to her and shoved his head under her chin.

Felicia immediately read her text.

Secure. Okay to open the door. Jude.

But what if Aaron had gotten hold of Jude's phone? Was she being paranoid or playing it safe? A selfie photo followed: Jude with a thumbs-up at the front door. With a gush of relief, she opened it.

Jude came in and immediately locked the door behind him.

"Horses were loose."

She found herself tumbling into his arms. "I was afraid. I mean, you could have been hurt."

He embraced her. "Safe and sound." He pulled her to arm's length. "You?"

She nodded. "Gracie and I were scared by the noise, is all. And Stretch started to bark."

Jude shot a goofy smile at Gracie. "I heard him, too. That dog is louder than a foghorn."

Gracie didn't return the smile, so he took a knee next to her, earning a slurp from Stretch. "Hey, honey. The horses got out and ran all over. That's all. You and Felicia are safe here with Stretch, okay?"

She rubbed her forehead. "I don't feel good."

Felicia came immediately to her side. "Like a scared kinda feeling or sick kinda feeling?"

"I dunno. I wish Mommy was here."

"Me, too. Mommy would know what to do, wouldn't she?" Felicia touched Gracie's forehead. "You don't feel feverish, but waking up like that wasn't real good. Does your tummy hurt?"

She didn't answer, simply laid her head on Stretch's.

"Let's get you back to bed."

Gracie's lip trembled. "I don't want to."

Felicia tried to think of how to calm the child. "Would you like me to sleep next to you?"

Gracie nodded. Felicia had guessed right. Gracie was terrified, like Felicia, and she needed someone close.

"Can I have a glass of water?"

"Allow me," Jude said in a mock English accent. "I know where we keep bottles of Death Valley's finest water."

That got a snicker from Gracie. Jude beckoned Felicia into the tiny kitchenette, where they would have some privacy but still keep Gracie in sight.

"I checked the property. No obvious tire tracks or footprints."

Felicia shook her head. "Horses don't run unless they're scared. Donkeys and horses wouldn't bolt from the corral just because the gate was left open. They might wander out, but not bolt."

"I understand. Could have been a mountain lion, a falling branch, a bag blowing by in the wind."

"Or it could have been Aaron."

Jude frowned. "Gonna be honest, Fee. I can find no proof of that. I will check under every rock and stone in the morning, but at this point there is no evidence of a threat."

"What about Stretch's reaction?"

"I was walking the exterior. He could easily have been barking at me."

She chewed her lip. "I really want to believe that."

"You can believe that you're safe right now. I'm here. I'm armed. Stretch is here, and Fox is driving the access road." He reached out and stroked her forearm.

Safe, she repeated. *Jude is here.*

She forced a breath in and out. "All right. I should see if I can get Gracie to bed."

He let his fingers fall away, and she missed the warmth, the strength.

"Your uncle's getting his stable hand up to help retrieve the horses. It's possible the gate was improperly closed and they bolted. They've had similar problems before. The two donkeys are still in their corral, all secure." He took out a bottle of water from the fridge. "Shall we get our little sweetheart back to bed?"

Our? He seemed to realize what he'd said. "I meant… I mean, she's a special girl and it's been, you know, a privilege to be around her."

She smiled up at him, noting the dusky flush to his cheeks. "I get it."

He cracked open the water and handed it to Gracie. "Here you go, honey. Good thing I didn't have to climb to the top of a mountain to get you this fresh spring water. Came right out of the refrigerator. Can you believe it?"

Gracie laughed and drank the water halfway. Jude capped it and returned it to the fridge while Felicia led Gracie and Stretch back to their bedroom.

"Good night," Felicia whispered to Jude from the bedroom door. "And...thank you for being here."

She could not quite read his expression in the dim light, but there was something soft and tender in his answer.

"There's nowhere in the world I would rather be," he said.

FOURTEEN

Jude took the phone call on the cabin's front porch, leaving the door cracked. The air was lusciously cool at a few minutes before 7:00 a.m., and he let it soothe him in spite of the angry tone of the caller. It typically did not bother him if someone else was unhappy with his actions, if he knew them to be justified. Except where Felicia was concerned.

"You're not supposed to be on this case, Jude," Detweiler snapped. "And don't give me the vacation excuse. Why are you at the campground with Felicia?"

"You know why."

"And you know what I told you before. You've crossed the line on this case. I'm telling you this for the last time. Let Fox handle it."

He waited for the rest of her ultimatum. From inside the cabin, he heard Felicia rummaging in the cupboards.

Detweiler sighed. "You're a good sheriff, Jude, but I can't have you mucking up an investigation because of personal involvement. Stand down on this or you'll be suspended. Am I making myself clear?"

"Suspended?" He bridled but kept his tone level. "Yes, ma'am. May I ask if there have been any further findings on Keira Mattingly's death?"

"No final coroner report yet, but we've impounded her car. We have a witness who saw her arguing with a man at Steel Rock Point, but they can't identify Aaron or his vehicle. Possible he offered to meet her, pushed her over. There might have been another witness, but we haven't located him yet. So you see we actually are making progress on this case without your help. Turns out we do have some other competent officers besides yourself."

"I…" He heaved out a breath. "I apologize, ma'am. I've been out of line."

She exhaled. "I accept your apology. We can salvage this situation. I've got everyone I can spare working on it. Enjoy your vacation, Sheriff, and stay out of trouble."

"Yes, ma'am." He disconnected, went inside and found Felicia waiting for a kettle to boil.

He took a seat and she stared him down. "I

heard the word *suspended*. That was Detweiler, wasn't it? She wants you to step out of my situation."

"She might have suggested something along those lines."

No smile, eyes sparking with fire under the fringe of lashes. "Jude, you could *lose your job*." She punctuated the last three words.

He didn't deny it. Instead he stayed bathed in that gorgeous gaze. "It's a risk I'm willing to take."

"Why? Your job is everything to you."

He didn't answer for a couple of moments. Planning out carefully what he should say, he opened his mouth, and something else tumbled out. "No, it's not."

"I think it is. You see the world from behind a badge."

He sensed her hesitation. "There's more you want to tell me. Say it."

She straightened as if coming to a decision. "And your badge helps you avoid things you don't want to feel."

A flash of anger burned once more, but a smaller flame than last time. "Are you pushing that dad thing again? I'm afraid of becoming him, so I stick to my job and don't connect with people?"

"Not with women, not deeply. Am I wrong?" She searched his face. "You deal in evidence. Show me some that indicates you've opened up, truly opened up to a woman about your past, your wounds, your fears."

"Felicia…" Then, after a moment, he blew out a breath. "All right. My dad betrayed my mom and plenty of other women. It hurts when you compare the two of us. That's opening up to you, right?" Man, that sounded sappy and he wished he could snatch back the words. This was ridiculous. They were in the middle of a threat situation, not a Dr. Phil show. He got up and fiddled with the window blinds.

"But, Jude, don't you see that the comparison to your father is proof?"

He darted a look at her. "Proof of what?"

She came close, put her hand on his forearm. "That you aren't him. You have a deep-seated integrity. You're a man who cares for his mother, his sister…" She punctuated each word with a little squeeze. "For me and Gracie. You're not your father, and you don't have to be scared of becoming him."

Not your father. The emotion that surged through him made him weak. He did not want to feel that way in front of her or anyone. "I… Uh, okay. Thanks for saying that."

"Our time here is going to end soon, one way or another. I figured if I didn't say it now, I never would. I really do want the best for you, Jude."

What if the best for him was her? A light flickered through his soul before the darkness snuffed it out. And he'd thrown what they had away. "Anyway..." He cleared his throat. "I'm committed until this case is wrapped up. Aaron will be arrested. I'm going to take whatever punishment Detweiler feels is necessary if I have to. God gave me this badge for a reason, and I'm going to live up to it one way or another." He walked out of the kitchen, feeling the weight of her gaze, heavy as her disappointment.

Outside, he strode around the perimeter of the house, trying to focus on his work, but the conversational aftermath intruded. He could face down any criminal, accept personal hardship, make whatever career sacrifices were required, but he could not wrestle with the onslaught of feelings Felicia made him experience when she'd compared him to his father.

What's wrong with me, Lord? Am I really keeping myself safe from relationships because I'm scared I'll become my father? With a surge of sorrow, he wondered if he'd ever know.

He'd better stick to being a cop. It truly was all he had.

* * *

Gracie seemed to be feeling okay, but Felicia kept a cautious eye on her. Another family had checked in to camp—a mother, father and their child who used a wheelchair to traverse the grounds. The two kids met up at the swimming pool. The doctor had okayed Gracie to wade but not outright swim, so she and her new friend sat on the steps and splashed to their hearts' content, with parents and Felicia keeping close watch over them. Stretch wanted to cannonball in, but he had to be satisfied sitting in the shade with Felicia since it wasn't a dog-friendly pool. The laughing children almost made Felicia forget about the fright from the night before, but she stole glances at everyone who approached. A few staff members, the camp lifeguard, her uncle. No one threatening. *Aaron's not here*, she told herself firmly. But had he been the previous night?

Then her mind rolled again to her unsettling conversation with Jude. She figured she'd made another mistake speaking her mind. Why couldn't she keep her advice to herself? He wasn't hers to care for, to worry about. And she felt terrible knowing she'd hurt him with her unwanted insight. Again.

Dan Wheatly arrived after lunch, his driver

choosing to stroll the grounds while they talked in the cabin. "Brought some supplies for the artist." Dan offered Gracie a bag with a sketch pad and a set of new crayons.

Gracie beamed. "Thank you. I'll draw you a picture." Then she frowned, glancing at his white cane. "Oh."

He laughed. "I can see a tiny bit and I use my phone to make things look real big. And I'll be able to see your picture if you use lots of colors."

"I'll use the greens and blues and some reds," she said solemnly before she skipped off to the bedroom with Stretch.

They sat in the kitchenette and kept their voices low.

"The police know this, too," Dan said, "but I wanted you to hear it from me. Aaron worked for Starlight Trucking, as we knew, at the same time Luca did. I found out a bit more about the accident that made Aaron lose his trucking job. He said he braked for a coyote and hit a tree. That's probably not very helpful. As far as we can tell, Aaron was not privy to Luca's injury settlement since they were only casually acquainted."

Felicia got the feeling there must be more for Dan to have made the trip to the campground.

"Uh-huh," Jude said. "Did you sniff out any other info?"

"Nothing official, but I talked to the trucking company secretary who has since retired. She lives out of the area and she was reluctant to gossip, as she put it, but I explained there was a child's future at stake."

Jude leaned forward. "You've got my full attention now, Dan. Don't keep us in suspense."

"Deborah said she worked late sometimes and once she found Aaron pawing through the files in her inbox. She confronted him, and he said he was putting them back since he'd knocked them off while he was sweeping."

"Did she recall what folders he was looking through?"

"It was information on company settlements and amounts. The names were reduced to initials only for some measure of security, but he wouldn't have to be too astute to figure *L.S.* was Luca Silvio, especially if he'd heard of his injury. Lawyers' names were listed, too."

Jude whistled. "All right. So it's possible Aaron knew that Luca was coming into some settlement money."

"It would appear so. Three months later Luca was dead from a hit-and-run, and Aaron entered Keira's life under the guise of offering support." Dan shifted, cocking his head toward Gracie's bedroom. "Sure it's okay to talk?"

Felicia tiptoed to Gracie's room and found her listening to music on her headphones, coloring with utmost concentration. Stretch opened one eye to check on Felicia's arrival and then settled deeper into his own snooze. Felicia returned to the table and beckoned Dan to continue.

"It gets even more interesting," Dan said. "The car registered to Aaron around the time Luca was killed was a Dodge Ram truck. He subsequently traded in that vehicle for the one he now drives."

"Can we…?" Jude started.

"Unfortunately, Fox said the car was sold to the scrap yard. Interesting timing, though, right?"

Felicia's stomach went queasy. "So… Aaron might have been responsible for the death of both of Gracie's parents?"

"Keira could be your birth mother, too," Dan said gently, "if the DNA tests prove conclusive." He cleared his throat. "Regarding that topic. The social worker and I were able to locate Keira's cousin in Brazil. I believe she's reached out and made contact."

"What…what did the cousin say? Will she

take Gracie?" Cold and hot ran in alternating currents through her body.

"I don't know the final outcome. I thought you'd want to be prepared that she'll be calling you soon, most likely."

And then it would be final-decision time. Her phone rang. Pulse pounding, she checked the number. "It's actually the social worker right now," she said through a haze of confusion.

Dan excused himself to sit on the porch, and Jude made to follow him.

Felicia's pulse kicked high as she took the call. "Stay," she said to Jude. "Please."

He looked startled, but he nodded. She put it on speakerphone.

"Ms. Tennison, I wanted you to know that we've contacted Keira's cousin Anna in Brazil. She works as an accountant, part-time, and owns a small home with a yard. She's widowed, with two grown children."

Felicia waited.

"She indicated she would be willing to accept the guardianship if you wish to decline."

Felicia's heart rattled around in her chest. "But... Gracie would have to move to Brazil?"

"Yes. Anna said she would agree to take Stretch as well."

And there it was. Everything Felicia thought

she'd wanted…a good life for Gracie with someone much more experienced, a better mother than she could ever be. The weight of responsibility would be lifted.

Jude touched her shoulder. "You can take some time if you want."

"I… I need to think about it, okay?" she said into the phone.

"I understand. Would you be able to tell me soon? I don't mean to pressure you, but Anna will need time to make arrangements to fly here and take her back to Manaus."

"Tomorrow," Felicia heard herself saying. "I'll tell you tomorrow, okay?"

"Of course. We'll speak then."

She hung up.

"Am I gonna go to Brazil?" Gracie stood in the doorway. She'd been listening to the whole conversation.

"I… I'm not sure. Do you want to?"

Gracie shook her head. "No." She looked down. "I want to go to school here. And I like you and Mr. Judy."

The words froze in Felicia's throat. She simply could not think of what in the world to say.

"Hey, Gracie?" Jude said. "Felicia's going to think it all over, okay? But we don't have to sit around this old cabin and worry about it. Today, we're on vacation, right? Your uncle Abe said we can go see the donkeys."

Gracie brightened and headed for the door, where she found Dan. "Oh, wait. I got your picture." She dashed back to her room and presented him with a portrait of Stretch with an ice cream in his mouth.

Dan thanked her enthusiastically and headed to his car, where the driver was waiting, while Jude walked Gracie to the corral. Felicia followed on shaky legs. The day was hot and heavy.

Uncle Abe called from behind the fence.

"Who's ready to give Salt and Pepper some apples?"

Gracie went wide-eyed and followed Abe into the corral while Jude and Felicia watched. Stretch watched, too, bottom wiggling to join them.

Jude met her at the fence. "So there's another guardian option for Gracie."

"Yes."

"Do you have any sense of what you'll decide?"

"I don't know. I've been praying about it daily, but it's still so muddy in my mind. Now that I've got to make a decision…" She shrugged helplessly.

He nodded and rested his hand on her shoulder, still watching Gracie with the donkeys. "Yeah, I've been talking to God about it also."

She jerked in surprise. "You have?"

"Sure. It's a pretty big deal for you, right? I figured the extra prayer power couldn't hurt."

The comment touched her right to the core, that he would lift her deepest need up to the Lord. She stood on tiptoe and kissed his cheek, which startled them both. "Thank you. That means the world to me."

He squeezed her. "Anytime. Great that Keira's cousin will step up to the plate. Sounds like she could give Gracie love and stability."

She caught the hesitation. "But you don't think it's the right choice?"

"I don't know, honestly. But what I've learned watching you two together is that, whatever you choose, it will be done unselfishly, lovingly and with Gracie's best interests at heart."

A swell of emotion clogged her throat.

He heaved out a breath. "I wanted to apologize. I think I made you feel childish in the past, like you weren't as mature as me or clear about who you are because you're younger. Seeing you with Gracie, I realize I was wrong. You're the most mature, wise woman I've ever met."

She blinked in surprise, too stunned to answer.

Uncle Abe called out. "Mind getting us a bucket of water?"

"You got it." Jude strolled off to fetch it.

She reeled. Jude thought her mature and wise? And he'd actually apologized for dismissing her as too young. Dizzied, she rested her forehead on the fence and tried to steady her nerves.

Gracie stayed with the donkeys until the afternoon heat made her face flush red and they returned to the cabin. Felicia plied her with cold water and juice and graham crackers, which Stretch snarfed as soon as one hit the floor.

"How about a rest?" It worried her when Gracie did not resist.

Gracie groaned when she climbed into bed. "I think my bandage is coming off."

"No problem. I'll see if we can fix it up." She snagged the first aid kit and hurried to Gracie. "Must have gotten loose with all the fun you've been having." Gently, she peeled away the bandage. The scar was still held together with surgical tape, but the visible edges looked red and raw. Infection, she thought with a panic. Keeping her voice light, she said, "Tell you what. Let me have Uncle Abe come and look at it. He's a doctor, you know." She sent him a text.

Gracie bent her chin to try to see the wound on her chest. "Is it gonna go away?"

Felicia knew exactly what Gracie meant. She pulled the neck of her own T-shirt down to reveal the faint line of her surgical scar. "Mostly. Now it's just a tiny pink line to remind me that I'm strong and I'm healed. And I've got other scars, too, from an accident I had. I can still see them and touch them, but they don't hurt anymore. It's okay to have scars."

Gracie reached up to touch a fingertip to Felicia's cross. "I had a cross Mommy gave me, but I lost it." Her face puckered. "I wish I still had it."

Felicia had the urge to say they could buy another, but she knew it would not be the same as the one given by her mother.

Gracie gulped. "I miss Mommy."

Felicia swallowed and prayed she'd say the right thing. "I'm so sorry she's not here, but she would be very proud of how you're taking care of yourself and Stretch, too."

And then Gracie cried earnest, hot tears that rolled down her flushed cheeks. "Where is my home?" she sobbed. "Where are me and Stretch gonna live?"

How could she soothe Gracie's pain? Restore

solid footing to a child who'd been knocked down and stripped of her family?

At that moment of grief and powerlessness, Felicia felt suddenly filled with a calm certainty that she knew had come from the Lord. The right decision was clear as the stars at night. She took a deep, cleansing breath and steadied herself. "You're going to live with me, Gracie."

It felt like flying on the biggest swing in the park, exhilarating and scary, but somehow knowing you'd return to the place you were meant to be. She knew she was supposed to be Gracie's family, her sister, a mother figure, if that was what was required. She didn't have to figure it all out, only to take the next right step, and this was it. God was fashioning them into a family and He meant for Felicia to step in and make it happen. "We'll stay together, if that's okay with you."

Gracie hiccuped. "Forever?"

"Forever." Her own tears pooled.

Gracie's bottom lip quivered. "That's good."

Felicia patted the dog. "Like the Three Musketeers, you, me and Stretch."

"Are you gonna…be my mom?"

Mom? Was she? "We'll be sisters, for sure." *No matter what the DNA test says.* Felicia brushed at her brimming eyes. "I don't really know what to call it, Gracie, but I'm going to try and take care of you like your mother did."

"Stretch, too?"

"Stretch, too. When it's safe, we'll move back to the house with the yard for a while, and we'll get you into a nice school. I'll introduce you to my mother. I think you'll like her."

"But…" Gracie's face crumpled.

"But what, honey?"

"But I still miss Mommy."

Felicia gathered Gracie up in her arms and caressed her. "And that's okay, sweetie," she said around a clog in her throat. "God understands that our hearts are broken sometimes. Let's pray about that right now and tell Him how we feel."

Holding Gracie's hands between her own, Felicia prayed, and when they were finished, Gracie added the amen. When she sat back, Stretch licked a tear from her cheek, which set her to giggling.

"What's your name gonna be?" Gracie asked.

"My name?"

"Not Mommy."

Felicia understood. Gracie needed to make it permanent in her mind by fixing the right label on their relationship. "Oh, right. No, not Mommy. We'll figure out what feels right eventually, but for now, what would you like to call me? Just Felicia? Or Fee? Auntie?"

Gracie's face brightened. "Auntie Fee?"

Auntie Fee. A swell of fear ballooned in her. Could she live up to that precious name? Looking at Gracie's small, hopeful face, she nodded. "I like it. Auntie Fee it is."

Gracie wrapped her arms tightly around Felicia's neck. Felicia held her close, absolutely certain God had helped her make the right choice.

"We're going to be okay," Felicia promised. If Jude could capture Aaron, Gracie and Felicia could be a family. Now she officially had her own sister to fight for. She looked up to see Jude meet her gaze from the kitchen. He smiled and gave her a thumbs-up as if he understood the decision that had changed everything. A moment stretched long between them, his eyes shining as if he, too, had tears in them.

Uncle Abe arrived to examine Gracie's scar. "That doesn't look quite right. I'll rebandage, but you'll need to take her to her primary care doctor and have it closed up again properly."

Felicia nodded and met Jude in the hallway while Uncle Abe finished up. "A trip back to town? How will we do that safely?"

"Leave that to me." Jude pressed a quick kiss to her temple. "Congratulations. If I'm reading the room correctly, you decided to be Gracie's guardian."

She nodded, eyes brimming with tears again. "I've just become Auntie Fee. I'm half terrified, half elated."

"You two are going to be amazing together." He sounded sad, turning away. Back to her, he added, "And I'm going to make sure Aaron is put away so he'll never bother you."

Jude was already pulling out his phone. She hoped whatever he was planning wouldn't get him suspended. A surge of grief rippled through her. Her new future would be full of unexpected joys and hardships, but Jude wouldn't be privy to any of it.

His choice.

His lonely choice.

FIFTEEN

Jude kept sneaking peeks at Gracie and Stretch in the back seat as they rattled away from the campground in his Suburban.

Gracie and Felicia were going to be a family. He couldn't be prouder of Felicia or more thrilled for Gracie. He'd gotten teary himself as he'd listened to Felicia tell the social worker her decision over the phone. An unfamiliar sensation expanded inside him, which he finally identified as regret. He'd had a chance with Felicia and he'd blown it. He could have been part of her life, part of Gracie's, if he'd made better choices, but his decisions had led him away, to a lonelier road he'd thought he wanted.

Like his father? He almost hit the brakes at that thought. Had he been working so hard not to become his father that he'd walked away from real love, just like Ron Duke? His mouth went dry. Not the time to wallow around in that familial mess.

When they reached the curb outside the doctor's office, Seth pulled his vehicle to Jude's open window. Nora waved. "We'll stay here as a lookout."

"We're getting real good at this," Seth added.

Jude nodded and turned into the parking lot, where he found Levi and gave him a thumbs-up from his truck.

Jude parked, feeling easier with his kin keeping watch. He opened the door for Gracie, Felicia and Stretch. They hurried inside, and the doctor took them to the exam room. This time Jude followed, staying with Stretch in the hallway while the doctor treated Gracie.

"Oww," he heard Gracie wail, and he and Stretch tensed.

The dog whined as if to say, "She's hurt. Do something."

"I would if I could, believe me."

Felicia's response was too low to catch, but her tone was filled with soothing tenderness. It cleaved his heart as well to hear the little girl in pain. How could he feel so deeply for a child he'd only known for a short while? But Gracie was special, like Felicia. The two deserved the best.

Better than you can give them. He shifted as his phone rang.

Nora sounded breathless. "Aaron just drove by."

"Stay with him if you can, but no dangerous stuff." He disconnected as the doctor opened the door. A tearful Gracie came out, and Stretch immediately conducted his own examination. She held him around the neck.

Felicia sensed Jude's tension. "What?"

"We should go quickly."

She nodded and they hustled to the rear. He stopped them before they exited, checking with Levi.

"All clear," he said.

Jude eased out anyway, going first to be sure Aaron didn't tear into the parking lot and try to run them down. He hustled them back to his car.

As they edged onto the main street, Seth honked the horn as Aaron appeared from a side street. Jude braked so hard Stretch slid half off the seat. "Get down."

Felicia bent low, and he looked to see that Gracie was curled up away from the window.

He texted Fox with Aaron's location and then he stared him down, one hand on his gun, as Aaron drew closer. Part of him wanted Aaron to stop, but not while Felicia and Gracie were in the car.

Aaron eased his vehicle by, slowing when he was parallel with Jude. Then he smiled and offered a sarcastic salute.

Jude's free hand was on the door, fighting the urge to leap out and drag Aaron from behind the wheel, but he knew how it would go. He had no grounds for arrest, no actual proof that Aaron was behind the threats to Felicia. Neither did Fox. Breathing hard, he stared daggers back at Aaron, whose smile grew wider as he began to laugh. When Levi pulled close in his truck, Aaron waved to Nora and Seth and continued on down the street and out of sight.

Levi called out his window to Jude. "I'll see if I can tail him."

Jude nodded as Levi drove away.

"All clear," Jude said to his passengers.

Felicia sat up and patted Gracie on the knee. "Okay, Gracie?"

"Uh-huh. Can we get ice cream, Auntie Fee?"

He had to chuckle. Ice cream would fix everything in the eyes of a kid, but he didn't want to risk a stop in town. "I saw a softie machine in the store at the campground, and Uncle Abe said they were going to test it out today on the staff. How about we get ourselves one of those?"

"The kind with swirls?" Gracie said.

"Yep, genuine swirls. Gotta wait here for a few minutes and then we'll hightail it back to camp."

Gracie agreed and they sat in silence. Seth and Nora cruised the streets in their vehicle. Felicia's palms were thrust under her thighs, and her knee bobbed, telegraphing her nerves. His were still jumping, too. Aaron's smug face was seared into his vision. Taunting him with his own powerlessness. After a solid fifteen minutes with the air conditioner blasting, he saw no sign of Aaron.

"Negative from here," Seth said via a phone call. "He must have left town."

Levi agreed. Fox radioed a moment later. "I'll have my contact report from the hotel the moment he gets there. And by the way, Detweiler said to call her."

"Copy that," Jude said smoothly.

Felicia chewed her lip. "You're going to get suspended?"

"You don't need to worry about it." He started for the campground. For a moment, he let that real possibility sink in. He might very well be suspended. And possibly fired for insubordination. Then what would he have? His life suddenly felt empty and small, like one of the old mining cars used to carry borax from the valley, left to rust in the desert sun.

Felicia looked as though she was about to retort when her attention went to her cell phone. "It's a text from an unknown number."

"What's it say?"

She whispered low, so Gracie wouldn't hear. *"Taking care of my little girl?"* She gulped. "How did he get my number?"

Jude gripped the wheel. "He's baiting us."

"Why? He doesn't even get the money if I disappear."

"What?" Gracie sat up straight.

"Nothing," Felicia said.

"Was it Aaron?" Gracie asked.

Jude hadn't realized Gracie might have seen Aaron before she hunkered down with Stretch. Should he tell her the truth? "Uh…"

"Yes, it was," Felicia said. "But he was just driving by."

"Is he coming to get me?" The fear in Gracie's voice cut right through Jude.

"No." He realized he'd snapped out his reply. "No, honey. He's not going to get you, not ever."

Gracie didn't answer, but he could see in the rearview that her eyebrows were crimped with worry. Not surprising that she didn't trust him, with all the trauma she'd recently experienced.

He settled into the seat, mentally seething. Aaron was going to answer for scaring this child if it was the last thing Jude accomplished. Suspended, or fired, he would make sure Aaron Mattingly went to jail no matter what it took.

They reached the campground. Stretch unloaded himself from the car, and the four of them strolled to the general store. Uncle Abe was there with his clerk.

"Well, hello, campers. How'd the appointment go?"

"It hurt," Gracie said.

Abe frowned. "Hey, you know the best way to put a doctor visit behind you is with a megaswirl frosty, and Auntie Fee texted me that you were interested in sampling one. Let's see if we can't make it happen. Chocolate and vanilla together?"

"Yeah," Gracie cheered.

Uncle Abe laughed. He and the clerk produced a cone for Gracie, but Jude and Felicia declined. They sat outside on a picnic bench in the shade. Gracie preferred to hunker on the porch step, as if they didn't know she was giving Stretch some licks.

His phone rang. "It's Bernie Youngblood." He held the phone between them. He didn't want to put it on speaker in case Gracie might overhear something she shouldn't. "Sheriff Duke, and I've got Felicia here with me, Mr. Youngblood. What can I do for you?"

There was a moment of hesitation. "I'm still not completely comfortable sharing information, but I've been considering what you said about a child being involved, and, well, to be honest, there is some self-interest at work here, too, on my part."

Jude raised his eyebrows and Felicia pressed close to listen. Her soft shoulder against his ratcheted up his pulse. He'd missed embracing her over the past few months more than he'd ever thought possible. *Focus, Duke.* "Sheriff Fox is in charge of the case, so you'll want to call him, but I appreciate anything you can offer me as well."

"I got a call from Aaron Mattingly."

"When?"

"This morning. He asked, or *demanded* is probably a better word, that I figure out a legal way to overturn Felicia's guardianship. I told him when he emailed me last week that it was not possible. He was belligerent, going on about how he should have been appointed her stepfather and the unfairness of Keira's codicil." Jude heard him exhale. "Frankly, he was irrational and threatening. I told him the law was the law. Felicia is the guardian, and it isn't in my power to change that."

"Did he say anything else?"

"Only that he would punish Felicia and then he'd come after me and shoot us down like ducks in a row."

He felt Felicia shiver and he looped an arm around her, tethering her to him. "But you weren't the lawyer on record for the codicil. Dan Wheatly was."

"No, but technically I'm the executor of the trust after Felicia." He cleared his throat. "That makes me one of the ducks, I fear. I recorded part of the call, if that helps."

A recording might not hold up in court, but it would be enough to arrest Aaron while they dug up more material for a case against him. "I appreciate you contacting me, Mr. Youngblood. I'll have Sheriff Fox call you immediately."

"I'd advise extreme caution, Sheriff."

"Absolutely." Jude disconnected.

Felicia closed her eyes. "I want this all to go away."

"It will." He was happy that her shoulder was still pressed to his, allowing her warmth and sweetness to permeate his cells. "Aaron's placed a threatening phone call to me and Bernie now, and he recorded some of it. We've got proof of a credible threat, and Fox will have justification to arrest Aaron."

It was merely a matter of catching him now. They'd be safe at the campground, and he'd find a way to ensure Felicia and Gracie were never bothered by Aaron again.

Ducks in a row.

Your hunting spree ends now, Aaron. Game over.

Felicia enjoyed watching Gracie eat her ice cream, but a chill remained in her body even as the afternoon shadows crept across the picnic area. When Gracie "accidentally" dropped the remains of her cone, Stretch managed to gulp it midair.

"All right, kiddo. You've had a super-busy day, so it's time to rest a while with some books."

"No swimming?" Gracie said.

"The doctor said not today, so reading it is."

Gracie sighed, but she hopped off the step and they headed to the cabin. Felicia knew Aaron was not at the campground. There was no sign of his car and Jude had already checked the cabin, but she still felt better once Gracie was lying on her bed with a horse book propped on her stomach. Stretch was only too happy to snuggle next to her and snooze while she turned the pages. Jude prowled the space, checking windows and texting. His profile was all strong angles.

Why did he have to look so handsome? Why did her memory stubbornly insist on recalling their laughter when he'd taken her on a picnic and dropped the pie he'd bought right into the dirt? Or the plans they'd made to visit the seashore someday and build a sandcastle? Probably the unruly thoughts were raked up because they'd been shoulder to shoulder lately.

No more. The hours were ticking down until Aaron was caught and they went their own ways. Gracie should be first and foremost in her thoughts and plans. Time to wash the distractions away.

"I'm going for a shower."

Jude nodded, his phone pressed to his ear.

She grabbed her towel and walked to the outbuilding as she'd done the previous night. A broad sweep of stars was peeping across the nighttime sky. Two of the cabins on the far side of the corral were occupied now. The campground would be bustling by the end of the following week.

Would she still be here with Gracie? Scared

of her own shadow? Or would they get word of Aaron's arrest?

And then she'd start the next phase of her life, the one where she was Auntie Fee, and Jude Duke was no longer in her world. She pushed inside the building and flipped on the weak light. The damp lent a humid feel to the air. One of the shower curtains was pulled shut. A thrill of fear coursed through her. *Run*, her muscles screamed, until her brain took over.

There were no feet showing underneath the curtain. She let out a shaky breath. *Paranoia, thy name is Felicia*. One of the early campers had come over from the far side to use the shower and closed the curtain after for some reason. There was no bench inside the shower area, no way for a person to hide.

Still, the niggling in her stomach would not abate. Best to be safe. Jude would not think her silly for an abundance of caution. He'd probably commend her for it. Gathering up her toiletry bag and towel, she turned for the door.

And found herself inches away from Aaron Mattingly.

He smiled. "Just like I told you. So easy."

Jude checked Gracie and found her and Stretch asleep, the book tumbled on the bedspread. He smiled and yawned. He could go for a nap himself, but not until Felicia was back from her shower and they were buttoned up tight for the evening.

His phone rang. Fox.

"Detweiler asked me to contact you. We've got a person who was out stargazing near Steel Rock Point the night Keira died. He took a photo of Aaron arguing with her. Got an APB out on Aaron now. Should be a matter of time before we get him."

Jude gave a silent fist pump.

"And guess what?"

"There's more?"

"Oh, yeah. After a lot of hunting, I discovered the car Aaron sold right around the time Luca Silvio died wasn't destroyed. It was warehoused at the junkyard, so we've got a team looking over it."

"Excellent. If we…" he started, then corrected himself. "If you keep the pressure on, you're for sure going to find evidence to link Aaron to the murder of Luca, too."

"Time will tell."

Jude knew what he had to do. "I appreciate the call, Fox. That was some really fine detective work."

There was a momentary pause. "No problem."

He clicked off.

They had Aaron now. No way he could wiggle out of this one. His nerves prickled. He looked out the front window at the shower room. No sign of trouble, but a pinch deep in the pit of his stomach made him uneasy.

Uncle Abe was across the corral at the stables. He opened the door and called him over.

"Stay with Gracie a minute?"

Abe blinked. "Sure. What's wrong?"

"Probably nothing, but lock the door anyway."

As he got closer to the shower building, he listened. No sound of water rushing through the old pipes.

His gaze traveled to the dry dirt and the heel of a shoe pressed into the soil. He looked closer. No way it could be the imprint of Felicia's flip-flop.

With a flash of adrenaline, he knew exactly who had left the print.

SIXTEEN

With Aaron standing between her and the only exit, Felicia had no choice but to retreat until her hip impacted the sink. *Scream, run, do something*, her brain commanded.

She sucked in a breath, but he was already lunging toward her, so she ducked his hooking arm and scuttled to the other side of the room.

"Help," she got out before he reached her, pinning her against the wall with his arm over her throat. Reflexively, she clawed at him to reduce the pressure. His breath was tainted with alcohol, sweat speckling his brow.

"No, no, Felicia. No yelling for help from your big brawny sheriff. I've been so patient, waiting around for you. I knew you'd turn up here at some point. Let the horses go on my last visit so I could snag myself a disguise. Do you like it?" She realized he was wearing a staff shirt with the Sidewinder Springs Campground logo, one he must have snatched from the laundry room. Clever. Anyone finding him there would assume he was an employee restocking supplies.

"You're not going to gain anything by hurting me," she gasped. "You still won't get Gracie or her money. The judge won't grant you guardianship."

He laughed. "Thanks for being so concerned about my situation, but since you're gonna die, you don't need to worry about my problems. You've messed up my life enough."

She yanked up her knee and drove it into his stomach. He lurched back and she raced for the door, but he snagged her ankle and sent her crashing to the tile. She tried to crawl away, donkey-kicking at his head, but he held fast.

"You're gonna die today," Aaron panted. "It'll be the last thing I do before I get out of this dump."

Felicia screamed for help as loudly as she could. The door burst open and Jude slammed in, gun drawn.

Aaron released her leg. She scrambled to her feet but felt a vicious shove to her back, which sent her flying toward Jude. He caught her with one arm, preventing her head from impacting the wall, but they both stumbled.

The move was enough to give Aaron a clear path toward the exit. The door squealed as he escaped.

Jude put her on her feet and charged the threshold, aiming into the courtyard. But he did not fire. She understood. There could be campers taking a stroll in the desert air, children. After a moment he called to her. "Are you hurt?"

"No." Her pulse pounded like a kicking horse.

"Stay with Gracie and call Fox. I'm going after Aaron."

"Jude…"

He half turned toward her, his body straining to start pursuit. "He's done," Jude snapped. "This is where it all ends."

"Don't let him hurt you." Something very much like love swelled inside her for Jude. Love, and sadness that he wasn't hers anymore. Maybe he never had been. *Lord, keep him safe.*

Jude held still, as if they were tethered together for a moment, and then he sprinted in the direction Aaron had taken toward the tangle of trees.

Felicia hurried to the cabin, her shin aching and throat still tight. Uncle Abe opened the door, wild-eyed. He drew her inside and clutched her tight. She managed to tell him in fits and starts what had happened. They sat together. He made her tea, which she didn't drink, and later he fixed a snack of cheese and crackers for Gracie.

Gracie's eyes were puffy with sleep. "Where's Mr. Judy?"

"He's…taking care of some business." Felicia hoped her tone was sufficiently perky.

Gracie pointed to Felicia's wrist. "You got a cut."

Felicia examined the spot, not realizing she'd been injured. "Just a small one, like a paper cut."

Uncle Abe got the first aid kit down from the shelf. "Always keep one of these babies in every cabin for good reason. We'll have you all fixed on in a jiffy."

But after he cleaned the wound, it was Gracie who took the bandage from the kit. "I can do it." She smoothed the bandage carefully over the spot. "Mommy taught me how."

Felicia could not hold in the tears anymore. She cried for Gracie, for herself and for the mother they might both have lost, for the misplaced anger of a man who'd turned killer, and for Jude, who carried her heart along with him.

Gracie hugged her. "It's okay, Auntie Fee. It's okay to cry. Do you want to tell God about it?"

Felicia was struck dumb by the sweet offering of faith, innocent and wondrous, all the more precious because it was given by a child.

Felicia held her hands and together they prayed.

Jude wished he could run as fast as Aaron, but the guy didn't have as many miles on him as Jude did. His knee throbbed as he sprinted toward the trees backing the camp. The ground was uneven and rocky, which almost caused a couple of crashes, one ending in a skid that tore the knee of his jeans.

He'd taken only one minute to alert Fox, who was responding code three, along with Detweiler. Rocks crunched under his feet until he reached the tree line. Heart thundering, he tried to still his breathing and listen. He'd lost visual on Aaron several moments before.

Detweiler texted: Roadblock secure. Got a second officer covering the fire trail.

The two main routes in and out of the campground were sealed off. So Aaron wasn't going to be escaping in a car, even if he'd gotten one stashed somewhere. He texted them both his location.

ETA two minutes, Fox replied.

Copy that.

He pulled his weapon and waded farther into the woods. Dry leaves cracked under his feet no matter how much stealth he attempted.

Something scurried to his left. Small, a lizard probably. Startled by an intruder? He activated his flashlight, cupping his hand around the beam. A swath of broken branches blazed like a beacon.

"No more hide-and-seek, Aaron." He flicked off the light.

Ahead he could barely make out a ragged pile of rocks. Had to be Aaron's hiding place. The guy couldn't keep running forever. Jude eased closer. Would Aaron fight or flee when Jude found him? Didn't matter. He was going to jail one way or another.

A rock crunched under Jude's boot and he froze.

Three seconds, five, and he inched closer.

An engine roared to life. Jude leaped back against the rock as Aaron surged by atop a sleek motorbike, the kind supremely suited for rough terrain. Jude took aim, but Aaron kicked out a boot, catching him in the cheekbone. Pain seared through him, but he managed to grab at Aaron's pant leg, gripping tight, wishing he had hold of an arm or a leg to wrest him from the driver's seat.

For a moment, he thought he'd managed the feat, but the bike pulled away. Jude lost his balance, watching from the ground as Aaron gunned it, weaving away in and out of the trees. Jude got to his feet, holstered his gun and texted Fox.

He tried to think logically. Fox or Detweiler would get Aaron. His hotel room was being watched. If he tried to get back to his house in Las Vegas, he'd be caught. The desert was vast, but the resources weren't. Even if Aaron escaped temporarily, he'd need gas, money, food. Jude knew Aaron would be arrested, but his own ego had demanded that he'd be the one to do it.

That chance had just dried up.

But Felicia was safe and so was Gracie. In a matter of hours, Felicia could close the chapter on Aaron Mattingly.

And on Jude Duke.

Dejectedly, he trudged through the mesquite-scented air.

That was what he'd wanted.

Why he'd broken up with her.

So how come it felt so wrong?

Felicia set a glass of water in front of Jude, which he drained. Mechanically, she picked a leaf from his hair. He didn't seem to notice. Uncle Abe had gone to read Gracie and Stretch a story, leaving Jude and Felicia alone at the kitchen table.

"I couldn't get him. If I'd been a little faster…"

"You did your best."

"My best wasn't good enough."

"It was good enough to save me." Recalling her terror in the shower room made her throat convulse.

His eyes darkened to a deep indigo. "Are you all right? Really?"

She tried to speak but nothing would come out. He stood and went to her, embraced her tightly and rocked her gently from side to side. "I'm sorry, Fee. You shouldn't have had to endure that. I'm so sorry."

He wasn't fixing things, trying to logic her out of her fear. He simply gave her the freedom to feel it within the safety of his arms. They went to the sofa, and he cuddled her to his side, draping a blanket over her legs. "I'll be right here with you."

She finished the sentence: *until Aaron is caught*. Fatigue engulfed her whole body, and she had no more strength to fight it. She fell asleep with her head on his shoulder.

* * *

She didn't remember exactly when she'd moved in the night, but somehow she'd packed herself to bed, waking as the morning sunlight peeped around the edges of the curtain.

Aaron... she thought, jackknifing up. The man who wanted to murder her was still out there. Or was he? Maybe he'd been apprehended in the night. After throwing on clothes, raking her fingers through her pixie and brushing her teeth, she found Gracie sleeping. Stretch lay across her feet, his head drooping over one side of the mattress and his legs the other. She left them to their snooze and found Jude in the kitchen on his cell phone.

His face went slack with shock. Whatever it was had been enough to rattle him. She hugged herself, waiting.

"All right. Thanks." He disconnected, silent until she could not stand it anymore.

"What is it, Jude? Did they get Aaron?"

"Not exactly."

She braced herself. He'd gotten away? Out of state maybe? Would she and Gracie be looking over their shoulders forever?

Jude cut through her thoughts. "He's dead."

She gaped, thinking she'd misheard. "What?"

"Aaron was found deceased at a rest stop

outside Beatty." Jude stood and paced around the cabin before he came to a stop in front of her. "Too early to tell, but he had alcohol in his system and an empty bottle of sleeping pills in his pocket."

She sank into the chair. "He killed himself?" How utterly terrible. Jude stood with his hands on his hips in a posture she'd seen many times before when he was mulling over a case. "You don't believe it was suicide?"

"Won't know the specifics for a while. Coroner's got to do their thing and so do the crime scene techs. Too early to tell. I have questions, is all. He didn't seem like the type to kill himself, but he might have realized it was a matter of time before he went to jail."

She tried to process the information. "Horrible. But if it wasn't suicide, who would have wanted to kill him?"

"I don't know."

They sat in silence for a while until Uncle Abe tapped at the door with a plate of bagels and cream cheese. "I figured after last night you would prefer to eat in your cabin."

"Uncle Abe, there's been a development." She told him about Aaron.

He shook his head. "What a waste of a life." He kissed her. "And a very sad ending, but I'm relieved you're safe now. No need to rush off, though. You and Gracie stay as long as you like. I have a camper with the sniffles, so I have to dash." He let himself out.

Safe now. She didn't have to stay hidden away anymore. And Jude didn't need to be her bodyguard. They could go back to being acquaintances only. "I guess that's one way to look at it. Aaron's dead, and the threat is gone. We don't require police protection." The words were light on the surface. Her breath bottled up in her lungs as she waited to hear what he would say.

"Yes. You and Felicia can start your lives together now." Jude shoved his hands in his pockets. "I... I'm real happy for you, and I'll always be around, as a friend."

As a friend. A cloud tamped down her feelings. His strange expression earlier, when he'd run after Aaron, had made her wonder if he could give her something deeper. Now she had her answer. Silly of her even to hope that they could be anything more to each other. He'd been clear all along. "Right," she said softly.

"It'll probably be hard sometimes. So we can talk, and if there's ever anything I can do..."

She cut him off. "I've done difficult things before, Jude. I ran away from this place with your sister, remember? We survived. I survived. I made a full recovery from being gravely injured. That's difficult. And I've decided to raise Gracie. It's going to be messy and painful, but I'll face it." Her tone was hard, but she couldn't help it. It was time to cut ties with Jude so completely that neither of them ever had reason to question it. She walked to the door. "I'll always be grateful for what you did for the both of us. Thank you, Jude."

He hesitated, as if he wanted to say more. Her whole heart quivered in those precious seconds, until he nodded.

"You have my number. Call me if you need anything."

And then he was gone.

SEVENTEEN

Jude figured he should call his cousins and sister and tell them about Aaron, but instead he'd sent a text. Gruff, probably, but he didn't feel like talking to anyone. He ignored their follow-up messages. The abrupt ending with Felicia would not leave his mind. There was nothing left of his mental resources to engage anyone, even family.

"I've done difficult things before, Jude... It's going to be messy and painful, but I'll face it."

So why can't you face your stuff? Was that what she was trying to say? His grit butted up against his pride. *I'm not my father. That's not what this is.*

Stalking into his office, he found Nora sitting in the chair opposite his desk. Inwardly he groaned. *Great.* Nothing like having your little sister around when you wanted to be alone.

"You're ignoring your texts." She crossed

one long leg over the other and arched a brow at him. "Well?"

"Well, what?"

"Well, what happens now between you and Felicia since Aaron's no longer in the picture?"

"Nothing." He shuffled the papers on his desk. "Look, I'm really busy right now."

She didn't take the hint. "Jude, I'm gonna be honest here."

"When are you not?" he said with a massive exhalation.

"It's part of that Duke DNA, I think. Anyway, you and Felicia are good together."

"We're not together, Nora. I told you that."

"You could be."

"No, we can't."

"Why not?"

"I…" And then the stubborn wall inside him collapsed under the weight of his need to know. It was too hard to look at her, so he got up and stared at the artwork on his wall, a photo of the spectacular Death Valley starscape, taken on a moonless night. "Do you think I'm like Dad?"

She didn't hesitate. "Sure."

It was a gut punch. He did not know how to respond.

"You're like him in a ton of ways. You love building stuff, you're impatient with people and you've never encountered a situation you didn't think you could handle, even when you are utterly wrong."

He looked at the ceiling and huffed out a breath, considering how he could end the conversation and get her out of his office.

Nora stood and he had to face her. "But there's one very important difference between you and Dad."

"What's that?"

She put her hands on his shoulders. "If you ever allow yourself to commit to a woman, you'll never break her heart."

He stared into his sister's eyes, her blue a match for his own. "How do you know that?" he murmured.

"Because God made you Jude Duke, not Ron Duke, and you get to decide who Jude's going to be. The guy you've chosen to make of yourself isn't Dad and never could be." She squeezed his biceps, then poked him in the chest. "So get busy, wouldja? Felicia isn't going to wait around forever, and she's way too good for you. So if you snooze, you're gonna lose." She stood on tiptoe, kissed him on the cheek and left.

He caught his stunned reflection in the glass frame that held his sheriff's diploma. The creases on his forehead and the lines around his mouth reminded him that he was not a young man anymore. Was it too late for him? His heart cracked open and something new rushed inside. God made him a brother, son, a sheriff, he'd always believed. It was time he accepted what his sister said, what Felicia had tried to tell him. He was not his father. And what was more, he was free to make the decision he knew deep down inside that God was spurring him toward. Hope sparkled in his soul. He wasn't going to wreck things this time.

He was hurrying to the door when the words pinged around his mind.

Wreck...

That nerve that had been twanging in his gut since he'd been told of Aaron's death nagged at him again. Quickly he returned to his desk and starting digging via his computer. He paused only long enough to dial Fox's number.

"Aaron's suicide is bugging me," Jude said without preamble.

"It's been bugging me, too. What are you thinking?"

"The wreck that made Aaron lose his job with the trucking company. It was..." He clicked his screen. "...about a month before Luca was killed, shortly after he received word about the injury settlement. Aaron knew of the amount and the lawyer handling the case because he was snooping in the secretary's files."

"Uh-huh."

"Long shot here, but what if Aaron didn't hit a tree while he was driving the truck?"

"Keep going."

"The person next in line for Gracie's money by default is…"

"Bernie Youngblood," Fox finished. "You're thinking he was working with Aaron to kill Keira? Then Felicia? Maybe he'd then give Aaron a cut of the money?"

"Possibly. Let's rewind that a minute. You said Bernie had a prior DUI. His bar was well stocked with liquor when I visited his office. He was Keira and Luca's lawyer, so he might even have been heading to the trucking company to arrange details for the settlement the day Aaron had that so-called accident. Maybe Bernie was driving drunk, ran into Aaron in his truck, and they worked out a deal so Aaron would take the blame. Bernie gets off without being charged a DUI, and he owes Aaron a favor, so they make a plan."

"What kind of plan?"

Jude closed his eyes and thought it out. "Aaron knows Luca is getting a settlement, so he pitches an idea to the lawyer that he'll kill

Luca and marry Keira to get his hands on all the Silvio assets, not just the settlement money."

Fox continued the thread. "Bernie knows every dollar and dime. Maybe he tells Aaron if he adopts Gracie upon Luca's death, he'd have direct access to the settlement trust fund, too, and it would all look legit. Bernie wouldn't get his hands dirty, but he'd get a cut."

"Or worse, they intended for Keira to have an accident like Luca did. That would leave Aaron with everything, including Gracie's trust fund if he was the legal guardian."

Fox whistled. "Couple of cold-blooded dudes. Aaron kills Luca and insinuates himself in Keira's life, marrying her and seeking to adopt Gracie." He fell silent a moment. "But Keira begins to get a bad feeling and fouls up the works by finding Felicia and appointing her as guardian."

Jude clicked his pen. "Since custody is off the table, they're going to have to go to plan B, steal the money through Bernie as the default executor after Aaron clears away the obstacles. Aaron kills Keira, then he goes after Felicia. He's the muscle, and Bernie stays behind the scenes. It all works until Bernie decides Aaron is a liability. Recording part of their phone conversation makes it look like Aaron was acting alone, but he knows Aaron will rat him out if he is actually arrested, so Bernie murders Aaron and makes it look like suicide. How would he have done that?"

"Easy," Fox said. "Met him at the rest stop with a supply of alcohol and dissolved a lethal dose of sleeping pills in his drink when he wasn't looking. Bernie left his body for us to find on the side of the road."

"He had to know we might not fall for the suicide trick."

"Maybe he just needed to buy some time."

Some time. Jude went cold. "I'm going to phone Bernie's office right now. Call you back."

"And I'll run his plates, check with the mechanics near the Starlight Trucking office to see if they repaired his vehicle around the time Aaron reported his truck accident."

Bernie's office phone rang ten times before the receptionist answered, flustered.

"Inyo County Sheriff Jude Duke. I need to speak with Bernie Youngblood."

"You and me both," she snapped. "He wasn't in this morning when I arrived, so I've been on the phone canceling all his appointments, which wasn't easy since I couldn't get into his computer."

Jude gripped the phone tighter. "Why was that, ma'am? Where is he?"

"He left a Post-it on my desk saying he was flying out of the country for a few days. Didn't tell me anything about it beforehand. Plus, he's changed all the computer passwords, for some reason, so I can't get into any of our accounts. Why would he do that, do you suppose?"

A terrible foreboding crept through Jude's body. "Please call me if you hear from him." He left his number and picked up the phone to call the nearest airport, alerted security there to detain Bernie Youngblood and faxed them a photo. He updated Fox.

The quiet in his office as he sat pondering was so intense he could hear the dripping from the watercooler in the hallway. Each drip marked another wasted second. Bernie Youngblood was dirty. He'd killed Aaron to cover up his complicity in the plan to steal Keira and Luca's assets. Now he was running. But something still didn't make sense. Bernie could deny everything, and if there wasn't concrete evidence to connect him to Aaron's death, he'd be off scot-free. So why run? *Think it through, Jude.*

Unless there was some sort of urgency...

Unless he'd decided to get Luca's money for himself.

Empty the fund before the cops caught on.

But it was Sunday, so it would take time. Nothing would happen until the next business day at least. Felicia would be notified by the bank of the withdrawals, so Bernie would be caught immediately.

Unless... His body went electric.

Felicia was out of the way.

Felicia knew she should feel more relaxed, encouraged even, that she and Gracie were no longer under threat. Somehow, her only emotion was sorrow.

Aaron was dead. Jude was gone. As she watched Gracie brushing Salt and Pepper alongside another child with Stretch looking on, she prayed she would be up to the task of raising her sister.

Like she'd told Jude, it would be hard and painful, but she'd do it.

Longing swept through her. She knew Jude cared for her, and for Gracie, but not enough to make him want to stay. Her uncle wrapped an arm around her shoulders. "You don't have to leave today, you know. That cabin isn't booked until Thursday. No need to rush off."

"Thank you, Uncle Abe, but Gracie and I have to get started on our new normal. She should be enrolled in school in Furnace Falls, since we'll be living there awhile with Mom. I talked to Mom last night and gave her some of the details. Of course, she's already planning to show Gracie everything in the area, from the movie theater to the sand dunes."

"That's Olivia for you. She's going to be the best grandmother Gracie could ever have." He kissed her. "And you'll be the best Auntie Fee, too."

After hugs and a snack and promises from Uncle Abe that they could return anytime, Gracie was loaded up in the back of Audrey, which Nora had delivered to the campground along with Stretch and their belongings. Gracie carried a supply of colored pencils and a pad of paper to entertain herself on the way. Felicia realized she'd forgotten to charge her phone, so she plugged it into the car and silenced it. There were several texts from Jude, but she didn't read them. It hurt too much to be reminded that she was a project to him, a friend to be checked up on, nothing more. Rallying her determination, she headed down the drive. The sun blasted through the windows and she cranked the air conditioner, relieved when they turned along the heavily wooded section of road. As they got deeper into the trees, the air felt hot, dense. The conditioner was not keeping up, so she rolled down the window, hoping a breeze would help.

Gracie rolled hers down halfway and stuck her fingers out the window. Stretch sandwiched his face through the gap, too, leaving drool marks on the glass. Felicia's brain trotted ahead of them, thinking out her task list. She'd call the school and find out what she needed to do to enroll Gracie. Then she'd contact Beckett and see about getting her job back at the Hotsprings with hours to accommodate Gracie's pickup and drop-off. The details were dizzying, and she didn't hear it at first.

Stretch did. At the sound of the approaching engine, he pulled his head back in and swiveled to see out the rear window.

The front fender of a car appeared around a bend, large, a four-wheel drive with big tires. Startled, she pressed the gas, but the car kept pace, closing in. She accelerated as much as she could, the wheels skidding.

"Gracie," she shouted in horror as the car slammed into them from behind.

Gracie's scream was choked off by her seat belt. Felicia fought the steering wheel. She almost kept the car on the road, but the tires could not maintain their traction. Her Ford plunged off the shoulder and bumped down the slope, coming to a stop inches from a tree. Dizzy, Felicia spotted the car that had rammed them on the road. In a fog, she heard the driver's door open. Fear knifed through her.

Desperately she punched the gas, but the rear tires spun uselessly. Jamming the car into Reverse, she tried again. Her car was going nowhere.

Adrenaline flooded her muscles, and she shoved her way out. Yanking open the rear door, she reached over and unbuckled Gracie's seat belt, pulling her from the car. Stretch leaped out on his own.

"We have to run. Find a place to hide," she told Gracie, as they tumbled over rocks and slipped on the sandy soil.

"Auntie..." Gracie fell to her knees.

"I'll help you," Felicia urged. "Quick, okay?"

"Stop," a voice said.

Bernie Youngblood appeared holding a gun. Bernie? Her mind struggled to make it real.

Stretch tensed, growling.

Felicia pushed Gracie behind her.

"Bullet's gonna go right through you into her," Bernie said casually. "You're both coming with me."

She forced the words out. "Why...why would we do that?"

"Because I'm going to kill you here if you

don't. It will be less convenient, and it will shorten my escape window, but if you give me no choice, I'll do it."

She felt Gracie clutching her around the waist. "We're not going anywhere with you."

He fired a shot that bored into the tree behind her, shedding flakes of wood into Felicia's hair. She screamed. The shot spurred Stretch into motion. Long legs churning, he hurtled toward Bernie.

There was a second shot. Stretch recoiled, whimpered in pain and collapsed on the ground near Bernie's feet.

"Stretch," Gracie wailed. She tried to run to her fallen pet.

"No, honey." Felicia held tight to Gracie's hand. The child continued to keen, great choking sobs racking her body. Stretch lay unmoving, and Felicia almost retched. It took all her will not to start sobbing along with Gracie.

"The car. Right now," Bernie said. "Or the next bullet's for the kid."

Felicia's throat locked tight in grief as she pulled Gracie past Stretch, trying to shield her from the sight of her collapsed dog. In a fog, she led them back up the slope to Bernie's vehicle. Could she run? But he'd shoot Gracie, like he'd done to Stretch. Screaming would do no good. There was not one solitary vehicle on the road save their own.

When they reached the car, he told Felicia to get behind the wheel and Gracie in the back passenger seat while he took up position behind Felicia. Gracie jammed herself next to the door, as far away on the seat from Bernie as she could manage.

"You're going to drive to Saline Valley, and if you do anything I don't want you to, it's going to get messy here in the back seat."

The valley was a good two and a half hours from their current location. Ultra remote. Largely untraveled. The perfect place to leave a couple of bodies. Fingers clammy with fear, she started the engine. In the rearview mirror she saw Gracie shivering as they left her faithful companion behind.

Felicia could not allow herself to grieve the loyal animal.

If she didn't think of a plan, they would soon be dead, too.

Jude figured he knew which route Felicia had taken out of the campground, since there were only two to choose from. She would have used the most direct one, the quickest way back to Furnace Falls and her mother's house.

Felicia. He kept picturing her wash of freckles and hearing her full-throated laugh. All the time he'd wasted trying to convince himself they shouldn't be together. The fear that she'd seen in him, clear to her as a desert moon, he'd concealed from himself. How ridiculous, how misguided.

He dialed her cell again.

Pick up. Pick up. When he got her voice mail, he disconnected.

Next he called Olivia's house in case she'd made it there, and then the campground.

"She left thirty minutes ago," Uncle Abe said, worry creeping into his voice. "Why?"

"I'll call you when I can." His gut knotted tight as he flipped on the siren and barreled toward the campground. The minutes crept by in agonizing slow motion as he bypassed the Sidewinder and followed the road she must have taken. His radio crackled to life. Fox sounded breathless.

"Not good, Jude. Bernie owns a small plane. It was hangared at an airstrip in Las Vegas until he flew it out sometime last night."

"Flew where?" Jude managed over his rising anxiety.

"Unknown. He didn't file a flight plan."

No flight plan. Jude's mouth turned to sand.

"Hangar owner told me Bernie hasn't made his payments. His plane was close to being re-possessed. Apparently he cut the lock on the chain-link fence, sneaked to the hangar before working hours and flew it out." He paused. "And a guy in town told me Bernie paid him a couple hundred bucks to pick him up near the springs in Saline Valley and drive him back to town. Gave him some story of visiting the springs and having car trouble. Guy didn't see a plane, but it could have been there."

"Saline Valley? He's after Felicia." Jude said aloud what his brain had already known. "He planned on getting rid of her and looting the fund before we figured it out. I'm heading away from the campground to see if I can intercept."

"Copy that. I'll arrange backup."

Jude's mind spun as he pushed his speed. A plane. Bernie was planning to escape in a plane. How did that change the scenario? The valley was a rugged, unpopulated area hours from his current location, where the occasional intrepid visitor would travel the dirt roads to enjoy the natural hot springs in solitude. The road he currently traveled led southwest toward the valley. But with a plane, Bernie'd need somewhere isolated where he could take off without attracting attention. His heart convulsed. There was a makeshift airstrip the locals called the Chicken Strip. It was non-towered and not depicted on FAA charts. Bernie could land his plane, capture Felicia and Gracie, and fly them somewhere distant. Fox would have known that, too, and dispatched backup there.

Or, he thought with a lurch, Bernie could kill them outright and take off, dump their bodies somewhere in the vast Mojave where it would take days, weeks, to find them. Some victims of the desert had never been recovered. A myriad of leftover shafts from borax and salt mines, wild burros and coyotes hampered searches on a regular basis. Inyo County Search and Rescue got calls every year from hikers who needed rescuing from the harsh conditions. Jude himself had driven Felicia to that general area when she needed to check on the status of a wild donkey she was helping Nora capture for Big Valley Donkey Rescue. They'd blown a tire on the uneven ground, and if he hadn't been able to fix it, they'd have been stuck there for hours in the ferocious heat.

Saline Valley had taken many lives.

But he wasn't going to let it be the end for Felicia and Gracie.

He was clutching the steering wheel so hard his hands cramped. He had to slow the car as he entered the wooded twists and turns. Why hadn't he figured it out earlier? Figured everything out?

Felicia was suffering again, and he was once more too late to prevent it. How could he not have tried everything in his power to make her his when he'd had the chance? Instead he'd pushed her away. Fool. And Gracie? The child who'd needed protection? Who'd needed *him*?

Lord, I've messed everything up. Please keep them alive. He hit the brakes and made a sharp turn that plunged him into a shadowy pocket of gnarled trees. A deep rut gouged the shoulder underneath a sprawling pinyon tree. Fresh.

He slammed to a stop. Gun in hand, he crept to the roadside to look closer. The marks indicated two cars. One had veered over the side; the other appeared to have pulled back onto the road at some point, the tire tread preserved in a layer of grit. Dread circled in his gut as he followed the path of the car that had exited the roadway. It didn't take long to spot Felicia's Ford, crumpled against a wide tree trunk, both the driver and rear passenger doors flung wide. His pulse bottomed out as he noted a bullet hole in the tree.

Please... he begged. Though he couldn't squeeze out one more syllable, God would know his deepest fear. On wooden legs he drew closer. He knew with crystal clarity that if Felicia and Gracie had been killed, his life was destroyed, too. They were everything, he now understood. They had been entrusted to him by God and he'd let them down. Unable to draw a full breath, he forced himself another two steps forward. Heart jackhammering in his chest, he checked inside. His relief at finding the car empty was dizzying. No women, no dog.

His cop brain couldn't rest in that emotion for long. They might have escaped, be hiding nearby. "Felicia? Gracie?" he shouted.

He was about to holler for them again when he saw the disruption in the woodsy detritus, the indication that people had passed by. A flash of green caught his eye from under a leaf. A colored pencil, Gracie's, dropped in haste when she'd gotten out or been pulled from the car.

Bernie had marched them back up the slope to his vehicle.

Jude wanted to rejoice that they were likely still alive.

But he knew they wouldn't stay that way for long.

He sprinted up the slope to his car. As he pulled back onto the road, a dark blur of motion snagged his attention. He practically stood on the brakes.

Stretch stepped quaking into the road. His head was low, sides heaving.

Jude leaped from the car and ran to the dog. Elation and worry warred inside him. "Hey, Stretch. What happened?"

Stretch offered a half-hearted lick. A small amount of blood seeped from a wound on the dog's neck. A bullet had grazed him. Another level of anguish flamed to life. "You tried to save them, didn't you?" He pressed his face to Stretch's uninjured side, fighting for control. "Aww, buddy. Let's get you into the car."

The dog whined, and his long legs wobbled as he tried to follow Jude. Jude scooped him up, struggling to hoist the enormous Great Dane. "You'll be okay, boy. We're gonna find them, but we gotta hurry." He wrestled the rear door open and deposited Stretch on the back seat. After he texted Fox, he paused long enough to wrap a bandage from his first aid kit around Stretch's neck. The dog sat motionless, quivering, his fur hot. Sweat poured down Jude's forehead after only a few minutes out of the air-conditioned car. The dog had been wandering for much longer than that. He spared one more second to pour from his bottle of water into a paper cup for Stretch, who lapped it eagerly.

Good sign. Stretch wasn't ready to throw in the towel, either.

He gunned the engine and they started off.

"We're going to find them, Stretch," he said through gritted teeth. "And we're gonna save them."

Stretch offered a mournful howl as they shot down the road.

EIGHTEEN

Felicia wanted desperately to soothe Gracie, who continued to sob as they drove, clutching her colored pencils. Unshed tears burned when she thought of what Bernie had done to Stretch, the gentle giant who'd been trying to protect his precious master.

Felicia wondered if she could somehow signal Gracie to leap out of the car, but how would she survive the heat? A tumble down the slope? And they'd been driving for an hour, farther and farther into the desert. The woods had given way to broad stretches of rocky ground without so much as a single other car in the vicinity.

"You can have the money," Felicia blurted. "The trust, or whatever else there is. I'll sign it all over to you or withdraw it or whatever you want, if you'll let us go. I won't even tell the cops."

Bernie sighed and wiped a handkerchief over his sweating brow. "Oh, if it were only that easy."

Felicia caught the scent of alcohol. "It could be that easy. The money is all yours."

"No. Believe me, I have no desire to kill either one of you. Murder's messy, and bodies have a way of turning up. Now it's a timing issue, really. The wheels are falling off the wagon, so to speak, since Aaron failed to kill you after he was aced out of the guardianship. Too many bodies now. Should have been easy. Luca dies, Keira dies, Aaron gets the money and gives me a cut. The codicil messed all that up."

"Your plan had to change to kill me then, too."

"Yes. You had to die so the trust would come to me, the default executor. That would have been simpler. Aaron might have been a suspect, of course, with all these bodies piling up, but he could have gone on the run and made a new identity for himself, and I would have funneled him some of the money from Gracie's trust." He sighed. "Aaron was immature, emotional. He became reckless, angry at you for messing up our plan."

Her stomach twisted. "You killed him, didn't you?"

"Had to be done. I realized that when he told me he'd called and threatened you, actually spoke to the sheriff on the phone. Ludicrous behavior. He would have tattled about me if he was arrested, I have no doubt, and that was a matter of time. I would never have partnered with such a clown if I hadn't crashed into him that day, but I had no choice. If I didn't cooperate, I'd have gone down for another DUI, and that would be the end of my law practice. I saw by the logo on his truck that he worked for Starlight. Told him Luca was my client. Coincidentally, he'd been snooping and knew Luca was getting a settlement. We got around to making a deal. Daddy dies, Mommy dies, Gracie's money goes to Aaron with a cut for yours truly. A win-win."

That explained the Bernie-Aaron partnership. *Keep him talking.* "What's the plan now that Aaron's gone? Kill us and take the trust for yourself? Like I said, you don't have to…"

"Nothing quite so neat. You and Gracie need to disappear, to give me time to siphon off Gracie's trust money without anyone alerting the police. You'd be notified of the withdrawals, see. All I need is twelve hours, tops, on a business day to move the money to my account and leave the country. They won't suspect me until at least midweek, maybe not even until they find your bodies, and by then I'll be gone. I have a place in Mexico. Not huge, but it'll do."

Felicia's skin went icy. "All this for twenty thousand dollars? I could get you the money another way. I have some savings…" she said desperately.

Unexpectedly, he guffawed. "Aww. You fell for it, too, huh? I fudged that amount. It's not twenty thousand—it's nine hundred and twenty thousand. The trucking company was negligent, and they paid extra to hush Luca up. Fortunately, the paperwork was sent directly to me. I deleted a digit before I notified Luca. Poor sap never even questioned it. He wasn't a numbers guy."

And he died right after the trust was created, courtesy of Aaron.

"Smart, right?" Bernie continued. "It was pretty easy to keep Keira in the dark about the actual amount, too. She was busy with the kid, and she believed everything I said. I am a lawyer, after all. It worked right up until she transferred the guardianship to you. So much harder when you were named and provided access to the accounting."

Felicia thought of the stack of paperwork she'd been forwarded when she'd accepted.

She hadn't even looked at it yet. But she would have, and Bernie's deceit would have become evident. Anger rattled through her at her own helplessness. "You're a crook. And a murderer."

He shrugged. "I have debts. It's not a mint, nine hundred and twenty thousand, but properly invested, it can keep me going. A man's got to do..." He let the rest of the phrase trail off.

She'd known bad men before. One had tried to kill her. Bernie wouldn't get the chance, she decided. There would be a moment, one precious tick of the clock, when she could turn the tables. She intended to be ready when that moment came. "Where are we going?"

Bernie looked out the window. "Far, far away," he said dreamily.

And when they got to the destination, he thought he was going to dispose of them like Luca and Keira and Aaron.

Think again, Bernie. I don't know how, but you're not going to hurt me or Gracie. She caught Gracie's eye in the rearview mirror and winked at her. Gracie bit her trembling lip.

Be brave, sister. We're going to make it.

The drive seemed endless as Jude sped to Saline Valley. Almost two hours had passed, and he'd shed altitude quickly as the car dropped into the massive arid landscape bordered by burnt brown hills and rocky peaks. Detweiler called.

"Lining up air support to cover the Chicken Strip. Don't do anything until we get there to back you up."

"Copy that." He ended the conversation. He'd do anything in his power to save Felicia and Gracie, no matter how outrageous the risk.

He eyed Stretch in the rearview mirror. "You hanging in there, old fella?"

Stretch lifted his head and shook it, sending his ears flapping. Jude was heartily relieved to see his improved alertness level. That big old dog held Gracie's heart, and he didn't want to think about what would happen if Bernie's bullet had hit something vital.

They transitioned from the paved road onto the graveled one that would take them to the airstrip. The landing spot was not for the faint of heart. Jude would never admit it, but when he'd accompanied his cousin Austin to the area, the 1,300-foot dirt stretch demarcated only by a series of white rocks had caused him to clutch the seat belt and hold his breath during the descent.

Puffs of dirt flew up from under his wheels, and he prayed he would not get a flat. He plowed over the rugged road, rocks pinging on the underside of his car. One edge dropped into a desiccated canyon. The bone-dry landscape released clouds of dust as they moved along. Bernie would be able to spot Jude's approach, unless he was distracted by other matters.

Swallowing hard, Jude kept on, slowing when he noticed tire tracks grooved into the shoulder debris. Bernie had left the road. Why?

Afraid to risk a flat tire on the sharp shards, Jude cranked the air conditioner and got out, quickly shutting the door before Stretch could try to join him. Hand on his holster, he followed the tracks as the ground sloped away toward the burnished hills.

He suspected Bernie might have ditched the car. He was planning on flying out of here, and he didn't want his vehicle to be easily seen in the unlikely event someone might be visiting the upper or lower springs. For the second time that day, Jude tried not to consider that Bernie might have already killed Felicia and Gracie. But leaving them in the car would risk him being found out sooner rather than later. Wouldn't it?

He found the vehicle parked behind a low cluster of rocks. Bernie had been thoughtful. The roof was covered with a camouflage-patterned tarp in tones of brown and gray that would blend in to anyone flying over. He flipped off the tarp, his relief swamping him that Felicia and Gracie were not inside. Tracks showed clearly that two people had passed by, one large male, a woman. Two?

Felicia was probably carrying Gracie. But how far ahead were they? He'd gone pedal to the metal, which had consumed some of their head start. He sprinted back to his vehicle, sweat pouring off his superheated skin.

Stretch had slobbered and pawed all over the window, which encouraged Jude as he jumped back in the car and hit the accelerator. *Hurry*, the dog seemed to say. *Time's running out.*

Bodies sticky with perspiration, Felicia held Gracie as they trudged. Bernie walked behind them, his gun ready. Through the sweat stinging her eyes, she saw the small four-seater Cessna parked on the dirt airstrip. A plan bubbled in her mind. First, a weapon. "Gracie," she whispered into Gracie's ear, "don't say anything. Can you put a colored pencil in my pocket?"

Gracie did so, silently, her actions concealed from Bernie.

First task accomplished. Now she'd put Gracie down, pretend to stumble, turn around and aim a kick that would hopefully knock him over. If the fall didn't send the gun flying, she'd stab him with the pencil if she could get close enough.

Not much of a plan, but the best she could come up with. They'd take Bernie's car keys and drive as fast as they could away from the danger. She wished Stretch was with them to comfort Gracie. She whispered again. "I'm going to put you down in a minute. Run and hide. I'll come get you when it's safe. If you heard me, squeeze my neck."

Gracie squeezed Felicia one time.

"No talking," Bernie said. "I brought some zip ties. I'm going to…"

But Felicia was already letting go of Gracie and whirling around, aiming a kick at his knee-cap. In her haste, she missed, her shoe coming into contact with his lower shin. He yowled and staggered back, but to her horror, he did not lose his grip on the gun, and she did not have time to strike out with the pencil. He swiveled the gun not at her but at Gracie as she galloped down the airstrip.

"Tell her to stop or she dies."

No, Felicia wanted to say. Bernie fired a

shot into the air and Felicia screamed. Gracie stopped suddenly, feet skidding on the dirt.

"Next one doesn't miss," Bernie said.

"Gracie," Felicia croaked. "Come back." Gracie must have heard the defeat in Felicia's voice, because her shoulders slumped and she looked at her feet as she returned and wrapped her arms around Felicia's waist.

Felicia murmured into her hair. "I'm sorry. We'll try again. Don't worry."

But her spirit quavered as Bernie pulled two sets of zip ties from his pocket. "Tie the kid's hands behind her back."

"In front," Felicia insisted. "She has a surgical wound, and stretching like that would be painful." Plus, she'd have a better chance of escaping if her hands weren't bound behind her.

He shook his head. "You really don't get what's going on here, do you?"

Ignoring the comment, Felicia looped the zip tie as loosely as she could around Gracie's wrists, each of the child's tears searing a path inside her. "It's okay. It's gonna be okay." *Lord, help me. Show me a way.*

"Now you, little lady. Put this zip tie around Auntie's wrists." He was scanning the airstrip uneasily. Bernie was not as confident as he appeared.

To her surprise, he allowed Gracie to fasten her wrists in front. Gracie slid one end of the tie through the other. Her brow crimped, and Felicia realized her clever little sister was intentionally leaving slack.

Good girl, Gracie. She felt a flicker of hope until Bernie reached out with one hand and pulled them tight. The plastic bit into Felicia's wrists. "Can't have that coming loose, now, can we? You're going to get in the passenger seat and put Gracie on your lap."

"Why...?" she started, then stopped. Because he would land or fly low enough at some point and they would be forced to jump, or be shot and pushed out. This could not be happening. She'd try to overpower him after they took off, but how could she do that without crashing the plane? She had no idea how to land an aircraft.

He prodded them over to the passenger side and opened the door. "Upsy-daisy. You first, Auntie."

Felicia imagined kicking her foot out, trapping his ankles and sending him down, but he kept far enough away that she couldn't. Panic dulled her senses as she climbed into the white leather seat.

"Now for sweetie pie."

With leaden arms, Felicia reached for Gracie.

She could think of no way out, nothing that would give Gracie a chance to escape. Gracie's eyes met hers, and she bit her lower lip.

I'm so sorry. So, so sorry.

Jude's car fishtailed as he floored the gas, laser focused on the Cessna.

Closer and closer. He shouted information into his radio.

"Wait for…" He didn't hear the rest of Detweiler's order. The plane had started to move. He had to reach it before those wheels left the ground or it would be game over.

"Hold on, Felicia," he said as he bulleted up to the aircraft, pulling around the passenger side. Felicia's terrified face peered out at him, Gracie on her lap.

The plane was still rolling slowly. Felicia pressed her lips together, and the door suddenly swung open. Gracie tumbled out. He braked hard to avoid her pinwheeling body. Stretch began barking, lunging at the glass. Jude hit the control to lower the window, and Stretch leaped out, streaking to Gracie, who had sat up, dazed.

The plane began to change direction, making a tight U-turn. He shoved open the car door.

"Stretch, get her in here," he shouted.

Somehow, Stretch seemed to know what was

required of him. He sprinted to Gracie, took hold of her sleeve and began to jerk her in the direction of the car. Gracie got up and stumbled after him. He yelled directions to Fox over the radio.

"The Chicken Strip. He's going to fly Felicia out. I've got Gracie and her dog."

"I'm almost there," Fox shouted.

When Gracie was inside the vehicle with Stretch, he put the car in Park and turned to her.

"Close the doors and lock them, Gracie. Stay inside the car and hunch down." He left the air blasting.

"Auntie Fee," Gracie wailed. "He's gonna take her away."

"No, he won't." Jude pulled his weapon and charged toward the plane.

Felicia saw an impossible sight—Jude Duke running, gun drawn, straight at the Cessna.

Bernie's face purpled in rage. He pulled out his gun and pressed it to Felicia's head.

"All right," he screamed, seemingly uncaring that Jude could not possibly hear him. "You want her to die? Keep coming, and that's what's gonna happen."

Felicia's own fear turned suddenly to rage. Gracie was safe. Bernie wasn't going to get what he wanted. Neither had the man who'd put a bomb in her car the year before, or Aaron Mattingly, in spite of his campaign of terror. She'd learned more about her inner strength and God's love lying in a hospital bed than she'd known in her previous twenty-seven years of living. Resolution and strength rose inside her. There was no way she was going to let this man fly her away to certain death, not while she had a breath of life in her. Jude was almost level with the passenger-side door. The cold circle of gunmetal pressed into her temple.

Her fingers crept to her pocket. She slowly pulled out Gracie's colored pencil and gripped it tight. Jude was now only a few feet from her airplane door. She counted.

One...

Two...

On three, she raised her bound wrists and drove them downward with all her might. The pencil punctured the fabric of Bernie's pants and burrowed deep into his quad muscle. He screamed, and she felt the pressure of the gun at her temple fall away. With a jerk, she yanked open the door and tumbled out. Jude scooped her up.

"Run to my car," he said, panting. The drone of a helicopter buzzed overhead, and a siren echoed through the barren valley. She did as he said, imagining he was right behind her until she heard the gunshot echo from the plane. Her muscles went rigid at the sound.

What would she find when she turned around? Stumbling, she prayed Bernie's bullet had not found its mark in Jude.

Bernie's shot was close enough to Jude's cheek that he felt the heat of it. No way was he going to give the lawyer another chance. He flung himself at the open passenger door. The plane bumped and jostled, so he had to hold on to the frame. It required every remaining iota of strength for him to leap into the cockpit. Bernie's eyes went wide as he aimed the gun.

Jude grabbed at Bernie's gun hand, and the weapon fired. The shot plowed into the roof.

"Get off my plane." Bernie's arm shook wildly. Jude was tossed off-balance by the jostling wheels. He shot a fist out, clipping Bernie under the chin. It was enough to daze him, and Jude wrenched the gun from his grasp.

"Stop the plane," Jude shouted. "Stop it now."

Bernie did not respond, clutching a wound in his leg and screaming at Jude.

Jude yanked the throttle down, and the plane came to a jerky stop.

Fox appeared, ripping open the pilot's door and leveling his gun at Bernie. Sweat poured down his ruddy cheeks as he glanced at Jude. "Oh, man. You scared me there."

Jude tried to catch his breath. "Yeah. My blood pressure rose a couple of notches, too."

"How about I take it from here?" Fox said. "If you trust me, that is."

"He's all yours. And thanks for the backup." He hauled himself out of the plane, trying not to show that his legs were trembling with fatigue.

Fox and Detweiler took charge of Bernie, cuffing him and leading him away. Two officers stood at Jude's car, where he figured Stretch, Felicia and Gracie were all waiting inside.

He heaved out a breath, bent over as his body tried to recover from the fight and the adrenaline rush. At the sound of running feet, he looked up. Felicia barreled into his arms. Eyes closed, he pressed her close, gratitude filling every pore and sinew. *Thank You, God*, ran through him like a funneling wind.

"Gracie okay?" he croaked.

She eased off and peered at him. "Yes. But you're bleeding."

He shrugged. "Scratch," he said, even though the wound to his temple burned. "How did you manage to jump out?"

"I stabbed him with Gracie's pencil."

He went wide-eyed. "No kidding."

She smiled. "It was dull, but he got the point anyway."

After a pause, he got the joke, and they both broke into unrestrained laughter. "Felicia, you are one of a kind."

"As are you, Jude Duke."

He saw the ambulance closing in. "You're about to get carted off to the hospital for an exam, young lady."

"And if I refuse?"

He didn't indulge her. "Gracie needs to be checked out."

She sighed. "So I'm going to have to be the adult role model and set an example?"

"Exactly. Raising a sister and all..."

"All right." He held her hand and they started to walk back, but she stopped, pulled him close, mouth quivering with emotion.

To his utter surprise, she kissed him. The kiss was everything she was: warm, gentle, exciting and shy at the same time. When they parted, he found himself speechless.

"Thank you for saving me and my sister," Felicia whispered. "Job well done."

Job? he thought as she walked away, leaving him reeling from their kiss. There was a message in that kiss, a thank-you with an undertone of goodbye. Natural. She'd forced him to confront something he couldn't, or wouldn't. He had plenty of excuses: he was simply a mature man, set in his bachelor ways, stubborn, jaded, closed-off and dedicated to a career that would suck the time away from a family.

All solid reasons, but not the truth that he finally understood. He opened his mouth to call to her, but she was swallowed up in a hug from Gracie, a joyful greeting from Stretch, questions from Detweiler and two medics hastening over.

Not now. Soon.

NINETEEN

Felicia granted Gracie's wish the day after the child was given the A-OK from the hospital.

"Can I please go see Salt and Pepper?" had been a frequent plea, and Stretch, wagging his tail, was in eager agreement. He, too, had been given a clean bill of health by the town veterinarian. Aside from a bare patch on his neck where the wound site had been shaved and treated, he was as robust as ever.

So they'd hit the road to the campground. Her body still went electric with fear at odd moments, when she allowed herself to remember what had happened. The social worker was setting up counseling for them both, and for that, she was grateful. She knew she would survive, cope with the trauma, like she'd done before, but she wasn't sure how to help a six-year-old work things through.

They arrived and met Uncle Abe for two

of his tallest, twistiest ice creams. The campground was fuller now, and Gracie found a friend to help her brush Salt and Pepper and offer them apples. As Felicia sat at a picnic table watching from the shade, Stretch sprawled at her feet, but he kept a wary eye on Gracie. Felicia, too, resisted the urge to check the area every few minutes.

Aaron was gone, she told herself for the hundredth time. And Bernie was in jail. All the real stuff, the good stuff, was right here with her uncle and her sister and her new life.

New life, she thought. But part of her felt as if something—no, someone—was missing. She pulled farther into the shade. *You have your hands full with Gracie*, she told herself. *That's enough. More than enough.*

She jerked in surprise to see two people making their way over to her table. The nicely dressed social worker and Jude, in worn jeans and a T-shirt, a baseball cap shading his eyes. Her heart jumped. It had to be bad news. Uncle Abe hastened over. He must have shared her suspicion, too, because he gripped her shoulder.

But the social worker smiled. "Mind if we join you?"

Jude nodded at her, friendly, reassuring. Maybe it wasn't bad news after all?

She waved them to sit.

"We wanted to tell you in person," the social worker said. "The DNA tests came back."

The air seemed to be charged with energy. Here was the answer to the technical question of sisterhood, but not the spiritual one. Her pulse slowed down. She and Gracie were family because God had made it so, not any piece of paper or blood test results. "All right. I'm ready."

The social worker continued. "Felicia, you and Gracie are biological sisters."

Felicia's heart felt like bursting. Uncle Abe gripped her shoulder. "Sisters?" he asked.

At first, she did not understand his question. "Sisters…not half sisters?"

"Not half," Carol confirmed.

Felicia let the information dance around in her mind. "So Luca was my father, too." The social worker nodded. "Keira and Luca had a relationship as young teens, which produced you. From what we can tell, they broke up for a while but got back together. DNA doesn't lie. You and Gracie are sisters."

Luca and Keira, her father and mother. The realization was twined with love and loss for the people she would never know this side of eternity. Keira had reached out to find her, the baby they'd given away. They'd gifted her a sister. Uncle Abe embraced her.

"Two treasures," he said, his voice choked with tears. "Your mother will be over the moon."

She felt Jude's gaze on her. His eyes were sapphires, shining more intensely for the tears she saw gathered there. He smiled, telling her without words that this was how it was meant to be, and he was glad for her.

For all the happiness, there was pain when she considered what she could have had with Jude if things had been different. She'd pushed him more than she had a right to, hurt him probably. But why, oh why, did her heart always drift back to him, this man for whom she could not stop yearning?

It doesn't matter what you feel, Felicia. He doesn't want you—not enough, anyway.

Wiping the tears from her eyes, she looked away. Hugging and kissing her uncle, she thanked the social worker. "I'll tell Gracie when the moment is right. For now, I want her to just enjoy the day."

"Absolutely. You have my number. Call me if you need anything." Carol left.

Felicia expected Jude to leave, too, but he got up and paced a few steps, eyes on Gracie.

She wasn't sure why he lingered, and she didn't know how to ask.

Finally she got up, too. "I guess I'll take Gracie to the pool. The doctor says she can swim now. I'll… I'll see you around, Jude."

"I've never been scared as a sheriff," he said abruptly, gaze on Gracie. "Did you know that?"

Felicia had no idea how to answer.

He continued. "Sure, I've had some moments of worry, maybe even a fright now and again, but I never thought of myself as scared, until you accused me of it."

Accused, such a bitter word. "I'm sorry."

"I'm not. It stung like salt on a stab wound, but it took that level of pain to get my attention." He still didn't look at her. "You were right. I'm sorry I hid behind excuses about our ages or whatever baloney I came up with to break up with you. The real reason was fear, like you said. I was afraid of turning into my father."

She wished she could make him understand. Tentatively she touched his arm. "But you aren't like him."

He faced her. "I am, in many ways, but not in the way that matters between us. I see that now. God made me who I am. I'm Jude Duke, not Ron Duke's legacy."

Wonder filled her soul. "I'm so, so glad for you, Jude."

He took her hand and kissed the knuckles. "I've been wrestling with a question, though. Maybe you can help me with it."

"If I can, I will." She saw his chest expand with a deep breath before he spoke again.

"What do you do with a woman who makes you better?" He held her loosely around the wrists. "Who isn't afraid to tell you the truth because she wants the most for you? And is courageous enough to risk being hurt in order to speak the truth? What do you do with a woman like that?"

She stared at him, at their joined hands, confused. "I don't know what you mean."

"What do you do with a woman like Felicia Tennison?" he said softly, his eyes pulling her in with their intensity. She was still mute, struggling to decipher his question.

He raised her hand to his mouth and kissed her again. "Never mind. I already know the answer. You ask her to marry you without wasting one more moment."

Did he actually say what she thought she'd heard? Before she could ask, he dropped to one knee, still holding her hand, and took off his baseball hat, setting it on the picnic bench seat.

"Felicia Tennison, you are the best thing that God ever sent into my world. You smooth out my rough edges. You show me what it means to be a selfless, courageous person. You manage your faith and your failures with more grace than I have ever thought possible. I still think you deserve someone younger, sweeter and way more tactful, but I am humbly asking if you will do me the profound honor of becoming my wife."

She stared, blinking hard to be sure she wasn't dreaming it. "Jude…"

"I love you, honey. I love you so much it hurts. When you aren't with me, I'm not a whole man. I need you, I adore you and I'll spend every moment trying to be worthy of you."

Tears crowded her eyes, and the words caught in her throat. She couldn't answer, but he tugged at her hand insistently.

"I'm not normally a patient man, Felicia, but if you need time…"

"No."

He drew in a breath, and pain flickered across his features. "No…?"

"No, I don't need time," she hurried to say, not wanting to distress him even for a moment. "I love you, Jude. I've loved you since the first day you came to see me in the hospital. I love you for every smile and every kindness you've shown me. Everyone sees you as a big tough cop, but I know the real you."

He closed his eyes and got to his feet, reaching to hug her, but she stopped him. "But as to the question of marriage…"

He stopped again, stunned.

"It's not just me anymore. I've got a sister to raise and, basically, to mother. You won't be marrying a single woman. You'll be marrying into a family."

Now she was the one holding her breath.

He cast a glance at Gracie, who looked over and grinned, waving the grooming brush. "You know she thinks my name is Judy," he said.

Felicia laughed. "Kids are funny sometimes."

"Like their big sisters." A smile tugged his mouth. "The way I see it, I've wasted a lot of time over the years. It makes sense to cut right to the good stuff and start with a ready-made family."

The tension inside her evaporated into a cloud of happiness.

A crunch snagged their attention. Stretch was busily destroying Jude's baseball cap.

"Stretch." Jude rolled his eyes. "That's the second hat you've ruined."

Felicia giggled. "So, um, you'd be getting a woman, her sister and a kind of unruly dog."

"More like a hat-gobbling moose."

"Are you sure you're ready for that, Sheriff?"

"Absolutely one-hundred-percent sure." He took her in his arms and pulled her close. "I love you. I love Gracie. I even love that monstrous dog. Marry me and I'll do my best to be a good father, uncle or whatever it is Gracie needs me to be. What do you say, Auntie Fee?"

Her heart went lighter than air, and goose bumps chased one another down her arms. Jude, her darling Jude, would be hers forever. They would be a family, with all the joys and challenges that entailed. He was gazing at her, waiting.

"Yes, Jude. I love you, and I want to be your wife."

He laughed, kissing her and pressing her close. "Wait until I tell my sister the good news. She'll say it's about time, and for once, she'll be right."

"I thought Dukes were always right."

"Oh, yeah. Of course they are. I forgot." And then he kissed her again, and together they turned to wave at Gracie…a new beginning for all of them.

* * * * *

If you enjoyed this story, please look for these other books by Dana Mentink:

Death Valley Double Cross
Death Valley Hideout
Undercover Assignment
Christmas Crime Cover-Up

Dear Reader,

I can't believe this six-book Desert Justice series is finished. I am content that Jude has finally earned his own happy ending, but I will miss the Duke couples, Beckett and Laney, Levi and Mara, Austin and Pilar, Willow and Tony, Nora and Seth, and now, at long last, Jude and Felicia. It has been a wonderful ride underneath those star-studded skies and across the vast, pristine landscape of Death Valley. I sincerely thank you for coming on this journey with me. Every sweet Facebook message, email and handwritten letter of encouragement has blessed me. I hope these stories of struggle and striving have blessed you, too.

Thank you so much for reading my books. If you'd ever like to reach out, you can contact me via my website at danamentink.com. There's a button there to sign up for my monthly newsletter, which is filled with fun and freebies. God bless you, reader!

Dana Mentink

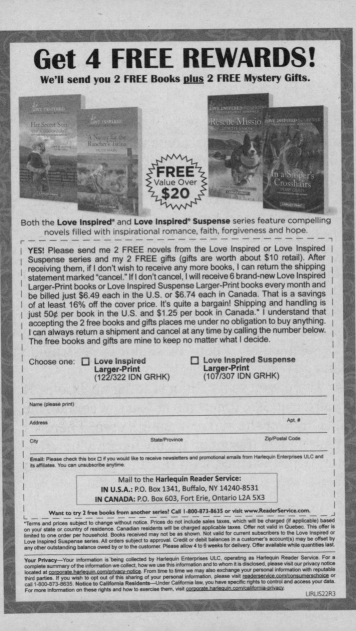

Get 4 FREE REWARDS!

We'll send you 2 FREE Books plus 2 FREE Mystery Gifts.

FREE
Value Over
$20

Both the **Harlequin® Special Edition** and **Harlequin® Heartwarming™** series feature compelling novels filled with stories of love and strength where the bonds of friendship, family and community unite.

YES! Please send me 2 FREE novels from the Harlequin Special Edition or Harlequin Heartwarming series and my 2 FREE gifts (gifts are worth about $10 retail). After receiving them, if I don't wish to receive any more books, I can return the shipping statement marked "cancel." If I don't cancel, I will receive 6 brand-new Harlequin Special Edition books every month and be billed just $5.49 each in the U.S. or $6.24 each in Canada, a savings of at least 12% off the cover price, or 4 brand-new Harlequin Heartwarming Larger-Print books every month and be billed just $6.24 each in the U.S. or $6.74 each in Canada, a savings of at least 19% off the cover price. It's quite a bargain! Shipping and handling is just 50¢ per book in the U.S. and $1.25 per book in Canada.* I understand that accepting the 2 free books and gifts places me under no obligation to buy anything. I can always return a shipment and cancel at any time by calling the number below. The free books and gifts are mine to keep no matter what I decide.

Choose one: ☐ **Harlequin Special Edition**
(235/335 HDN GRJV)

☐ **Harlequin Heartwarming Larger-Print**
(161/361 HDN GRJV)

Name (please print)

Address _____ Apt. #

City _____ State/Province _____ Zip/Postal Code

Email: Please check this box ☐ if you would like to receive newsletters and promotional emails from Harlequin Enterprises ULC and its affiliates. You can unsubscribe anytime.

Mail to the Harlequin Reader Service:
IN U.S.A.: P.O. Box 1341, Buffalo, NY 14240-8531
IN CANADA: P.O. Box 603, Fort Erie, Ontario L2A 5X3

Want to try 2 free books from another series? Call 1-800-873-8635 or visit www.ReaderService.com.

*Terms and prices subject to change without notice. Prices do not include sales taxes, which will be charged (if applicable) based on your state or country of residence. Canadian residents will be charged applicable taxes. Offer not valid in Quebec. This offer is limited to one order per household. Books received may not be as shown. Not valid for current subscribers to the Harlequin Special Edition or Harlequin Heartwarming series. All orders subject to approval. Credit or debit balances in a customer's account(s) may be offset by any other outstanding balance owed by or to the customer. Please allow 4 to 6 weeks for delivery. Offer available while quantities last.

Your Privacy—Your information is being collected by Harlequin Enterprises ULC, operating as Harlequin Reader Service. For a complete summary of the information we collect, how we use this information and to whom it is disclosed, please visit our privacy notice located at corporate.harlequin.com/privacy-notice. From time to time we may also exchange your personal information with reputable third parties. If you wish to opt out of this sharing of your personal information, please visit readerservice.com/consumerschoice or call 1-800-873-8635. Notice to California Residents—Under California law, you have specific rights to control and access your data. For more information on these rights and how to exercise them, visit corporate.harlequin.com/california-privacy.

HSEHW22R3

COUNTRY LEGACY COLLECTION

19 FREE BOOKS IN ALL!

Cowboys, adventure and romance await you in this new collection! Enjoy superb reading all year long with books by bestselling authors like Diana Palmer, Sasha Summers and Marie Ferrarella!

YES! Please send me the **Country Legacy Collection!** This collection begins with 3 FREE books and 2 FREE gifts in the first shipment. Along with my 3 free books, I'll also get 3 more books from the **Country Legacy Collection**, which I may either return and owe nothing or keep for the low price of $24.60 U.S./$28.12 CDN each plus $2.99 U.S./$7.49 CDN for shipping and handling per shipment*. If I decide to continue, about once a month for 8 months, I will get 6 or 7 more books but will only pay for 4. That means 2 or 3 books in every shipment will be FREE! If I decide to keep the entire collection, I'll have paid for only 32 books because 19 are FREE! I understand that accepting the 3 free books and gifts places me under no obligation to buy anything. I can always return a shipment and cancel at any time. My free books and gifts are mine to keep no matter what I decide.

☐ 275 HCK 1939   ☐ 475 HCK 1939

Name (please print)

Address   Apt. #

City   State/Province   Zip/Postal Code

Mail to the **Harlequin Reader Service:**
IN U.S.A.: P.O. Box 1341, Buffalo, NY 14240-8571
IN CANADA: P.O. Box 603, Fort Erie, Ontario L2A 5X3